Helena

By E. M. Brophy

To the Oxford Writing Guild for all their
support and cocktails.

And to mum and dad, for everything.

Contents

I. The Beginning

How does a woman give birth to an egg?

This is not a riddle. I'm genuinely curious as to your answer.

For myself, I have no idea. I cannot fathom how that would work, despite having birthed half a dozen children myself. Can you imagine pushing out an egg?

It's the latest addition you see. To the grander story. Though I suppose it comes from some truth. I can see the ingredients that were mixed, then expanded or compounded, the gossip and lies and whispers that were combined and whipped to create this story. And it makes for a good story; makes it more exciting, makes it make sense. Still this story would never really make sense. War never does.

The alternative is boring. Something so incredibly mundane and nasty, something so human and base, so obvious, that only the most extravagant lies will do. Then that lie grows and grows and becomes legend, until eventually it is said with such certainly, no one even considers the truth. And then they add to it even more. They add an egg.

I have often wondered what would have happened, how my life would have been, had that lie not been told, that suggestion not uttered. I suppose I'd have been killed. Either left on a lonely rock to starve, or my brains dashed out against a wall.

But what if I'd lived?

What if that lie had never been told and I had stayed alive. What life would I have lived? What would people have seen in me? How would I have appeared to them? Would anyone have gone to war over me?

Not that anyone really went to war over me. Men do not go to war over women, even if that's what they tell themselves. They go to war over power and ego, not wives. I suppose my question is more, would I have been used as I was? Would anyone have wanted me at all?

I'm rambling. I tend to do that now. The servant girls roll their eyes at me and whisper behind my back. They think I'm going senile.

I can assure you, I'm not. My mind is as sharp as ever, though that might not be saying much.

I find myself wanting to talk about the past. Not so much the recent past, but to revisit what happened to me so long ago, I could almost persuade myself it was a dream. Almost.

It hurts. So much of it hurts, and sometimes I find it hard to remember, or to focus on one time or place. Entef has heard it before, more or less, and he knows how frustrated I get with my past. He's suggested I write it down rather than rambling in half-truths to people around me. He thinks it might help with the pain, especially the bits that are hard to say out loud. So, I am taking his advice. I am writing it down, here, right now.

Maybe I'm not being driven by my own inner demons, but what's going on elsewhere, outside of my happy little bubble. The tales of the Trojan War, the Fall of Ilium, are spreading, growing, changing; they're a favourite tale even here, far from the action. They sing songs of Helen and

Paris, Achilles and Hector, of the wars of gods and goddesses being played out by heroes on the ground. But it's all so vague, even as a thousand different versions pop up, it feels less grounded each time I hear it. And it doesn't reflect me, or my life, at all.

To be clear, I have no desire to rewrite history or decimate legend. I do not have the inclination to retell what is told around the campfires when soldiers are far from home. To go into detail about camps and battles and rooms and clothes and where everyone stood and what everyone said and how everyone felt. How could I? I was not present for most of that story.

The only person I have real insight into is myself. As limited as our views of ourselves is.

I realise as I write this, that I have not told you who I am. I have just assumed you know. I've often assumed that though, that people see me, recognise me immediately. I suppose that tells you a lot about me. But that is another part of the story that has changed; I do not recall ever being called Helen of Troy. Even as I lived there, even as the palace burned around me, no one called me that. I suppose that name is close, fairly accurate to what I was called, to what I called myself, at least for a while. And the slight change of a name is nothing compared to the other changes. Or to the questions that name conjures.

I know you have questions; did I love him? What were the great heroes like? Are the gods real?

Was I birthed from an egg?

And so, I shall tell you; I shall answer these as they come to my mind. And if this should change your perceptions or cause you to look at a hero in a different light, then so be it.

Perhaps it'll change your view of me, or perhaps you'll end this thinking this proves I'm the vain, homewrecking, whore you always thought I was. But at least you'll be basing that on my story, rather than someone else's.

Perhaps all of this will be frustrating for you, reader, but I'm an old woman and I find I don't much care.

I want to tell the story of me. All the versions of me. Helena, Lena, Ena.

The face that launched a thousand ships?

That's what they call me. That's the moniker I am lumbered with. It was far fewer than a thousand – can you imagine! I don't think I've ever seen a thousand of anything. And it was certainly not my face that called them to action; how could it, most had never seen me. It had far more to do with trade routes and power and more than one crafty king who saw an opportunity to whip up a frenzy. But that'll come later.

But it is undoubtedly the question people want answering about me. What does she look like? Is she really that beautiful? A goddess on earth? Or is she plain, boring, no better than any other woman except for a tall tale? And even if she is beautiful, what of her soul? Is she cruel or kind, good or evil, a damsel or a seducer? As to the answer to those questions, I'll let you decide as you read on.

Well, what *did* she look like? What did *I* look like? Though I wonder if those two questions are the same one. I'm an old woman now and no one cares about my face; they turn from me in disgust. I'd thank the gods for that if I thought it was a favour from them, but I know it was all me.

I've occasionally heard the storytellers describe this most famous beauty. I find it fascinating what they say, and how it's changed over my lifetime. I wonder how much of beauty is caught up in the exotic or the familiar? How much do people find the unusual alluring? Was I actually beautiful or did I just look different enough in a pleasing way, in a way they value? Something for the philosophers to consider, I think.

I'm going to try to give you the basics, so you can visualise me, but I suspect the picture you conjure up with will be some other woman. I'm not offended. It's also been a while, a long while, since I saw that face. I mostly used to avoid reflective surfaces, rushing past them, splashing the water if it cast a reflection; I learned early on that how I looked was not something to be happy about. But I shall try my best to sate your curiosity.

My skin was dark, bronze even in the winter, turning deep brown in the summer. My hair was thick with tight curls that exploded around my face; it seemed to need little assistance, but I piled on the same ointments and perfumes as my sisters. I had plump lips, dark at the edges then turning pink in the centre, high cheekbones, a straight nose, and my eyes were bright green and shaped like a cat's. My neck was long; swan-like you might say (and people often have, with a wink). I've always felt it was my best feature.

I was average height, like the other women around me. My figure was full, with wide hips and a small soft belly, and full breasts, both bigger and saggier now. I was proportionate, I think.

So, based on this, what do you see? Am I a beauty? Or were you thinking of an Amazonian blonde? A fleshy northern red head? A pale straight-haired easterner? Do I appear as a rival to Aphrodite?

Perhaps you are already thinking how 'not-beautiful' I sound? Not even pretty, why is anyone interested in that? I heard that enough as well, mostly whispers in a corridor, though sometimes to my face. It's difficult to know if it was jealousy or the truth.

It's difficult for me to know how I saw myself, even all these years later. I have never felt my beauty exactly, I've never quite believed I was all that beautiful, but I always knew I was different, that I was perceived differently. Perhaps that is feeling beautiful? Have I felt the same when old and ugly? I suppose so, but in a different way; people averting their eyes rather than staring. Looks of pity rather than lust, shock instead of awe.

For me, losing my beauty was the best thing that happened. It helped me discover my voice, or if not my voice, then myself. I honestly spent half a lifetime not realising that. It freed me in a way I had never known.

Or perhaps it wasn't how I looked that kept me trapped, but the novelty of it. The idea of what that meant. I didn't look like anyone in the palace, anyone in my world. I was a wonder. I was otherworldly. I just don't think that world was a divine one. And now, I have come crashing back to earth.

Overall, it was confusing. Very confusing. To be praised and insulted, mocked, and ogled for the same things, which I have little control over. It's enough to make anyone go mad.

All of this leads to that other question. The question that is really being asked when you want to know how I looked.

Was I worth it?

Was I worth going to war over? Was I truly beautiful enough for men to lose their minds and their lives getting me back?

No.

The answer will always be no.

I know that for a fact.

Because nothing is worth that.

II. Sparta

What do people think of when they think of Sparta? They think of war and men and power, of strange rituals and rites, of ambition and arrogance. It is very different from how I think of Sparta. I think of quiet small hallways, of laughing with my sister, running from my father, weeping for my mother. I think of women, being surrounded by whispering women.

How can I describe Sparta to you? The Sparta I knew, the space I inhabited.

The palace was dark and low and labyrinthine; bigger and grander than the houses surrounding it, but perhaps not as much as you'd think. I spent my life in the women's quarters, my sister's and mother's rooms, at my loom, in the garden. But even as a child, Sparta felt small while acting big, full of war and conquest and slaves. Someone in Troy once mentioned that Sparta was richer than it looked, and I suppose it must have been. Spears often have that effect.

I find in general, my memory of Sparta fading, or faded, corrupted by years away and the views of others. But even as I sit here, considering my youth, I find myself turning from the word 'home'. I was born there, I lived there, I was Queen there, and I thought I was going to die there, but still, the word does not make me feel safe or nostalgic. I am sad for the people who I loved, the few I loved, who I lived with and lost, but not for the place or my place in it.

I suppose that makes sense; no one thinks of Helena of Sparta.

Daughter of the gods

Ah, the crux of the matter.

See how clever I've been! Starting with that question but delaying the details. I want to apologise in advance to all those who regularly offer something to the gods or have heard about the birth of Helena of Troy and believed it. I'm afraid you might be disappointed.

The legend of me can be traced quite clearly. Because it is already a legend. I'm not even dead yet, and the way the stories have travelled and changed, it has far outgrown me.

To many people, the year has four seasons: two of life and birth, and two of decay and death. But to men, especially the men of Sparta, there is a fifth season, one that can last years – the season of war. When the great and brave march out of their city to fight the next city or the next king or whoever they can find. It means that the kings and warriors aren't at home. They aren't there to lay the fires, to offer sacrifices, to bring home the hunt. And they are not there to father children.

I assume you can see where this is going.

I have no idea what was said, or done, how my mother survived the revelation that she was carrying a bastard child. Perhaps even my father quaked at killing an obviously pregnant woman? Perhaps the divine story was already unfolding? Whispers through the palace halls. You might not think such murmurings could change history, but they can. I wasn't the only surprise child who might have been given a story to protect them, and the men around them.

And whilst I was there for my birth, I'm of no help at all. I do not know if I came into this world hard or easy, if I had hair, what colour my eyes were, even if my mother used birthing bricks. All I can tell you, are the whispers that swirled around me, just out of earshot, as a child, but became louder as I grew, and since have morphed and changed into something so grand as to be unrecognisable.

At some point, someone said I was the daughter of the gods. A daughter of Zeus. Then, because such a child cannot come into this world in a traditional way, Zeus had laid with mother in the guise of a swan. Perhaps it was just a small comment, but it sparked the imagination.

I've heard that on the night I was born there was a great storm, but only lightning, no rain. I was told by a woman in the market that I could walk and speak after a few days, like no other human child could. I even heard a whisper that I had emerged fully formed, but with the mind of a simpleton. That I had been born with swan down, that disappeared after a few hours. I suppose cygnets are hatched with dark feathers. And, most famously, that my mother did not give birth to a human at all, but to an egg that hatched.

Or so they say.

And what can I say in response? I've already told you I can see the ingredients that make up the story; I can remember Sparta, I can look at the world around me, I can use my own experience, knowledge. I can think of what I might do. Perhaps there are some answers in there?

I have given birth to four living children and aided the delivery of a dozen more. I know that there is a sack produced after the birth. I once asked my own midwife about this; when I was in Troy and about to give birth to my first son there. I'd been too shy, too worried, too young, to ask them in Sparta. And I'm not sure they'd have told me the truth anyway. The midwife told me that, though rare, this sack can come out with the child still inside.

She did not think it resembled an egg.

I am not the daughter of the gods.

I am not even sure they exist.

And so, that story is a lie.

The why is obvious; someone wanted to save my life, or my mother's, or both. I can imagine the mutterings as my mother became rounder, the raised eyebrows as they counted the months on their fingers. I'm not sure even that would have been a problem though if I hadn't been born with such dark skin.

So, let's ask who told the story, who created the lie?

Perhaps it was my mother herself, laying the groundwork long before the birth.

Leda did love swans.

Traces of them could be found throughout the women's quarters, even after I was Queen, despite being faded or painted over. I once found a jewellery box hidden away full of beautiful things decorated with swans. And there once was a pond where they nested, along with other birds and animals and fish; she would apparently spend hours there, watching them whilst she sewed.

I say apparently because there were no swans after I was born. My father had them all killed. Any swan that came onto Spartan land was killed. All our cushions were stuffed with swan-down. Or so they said.

I suppose otherwise, it was some quick-thinking midwife or servant. Inspired by the weather perhaps. Or by other stories. I am not the only person with divine parentage. I wonder what their story is? Achilles for example, they said his mother was a sea goddess, but perhaps she was just a woman who drowned? There seem to be a lot of us, divine children, in the world, but how many of us are given this moniker to cover up the sins of our parents?

I gleaned all this from gossip, whispers and hushed voices, listening at doors and hiding in cupboards, usually with Nest. I am very good at being quiet, hiding carefully, and hearing truths I probably shouldn't. As I grew older, I heard the 'official' story, the story of Zeus, and I came to understand its significance, but otherwise I learned all this secretly. My nursemaid told me some, when asked, but the rest I pieced together. I've never shared it with anyone until now.

I suppose you want me to tell you about my father, the man that made me. That's the obvious question now? If not Zeus, then who?

I do not know how I was conceived.

It is a great joke that humanity insists on our past being the key to our future, and yet most of us have no idea what lay in our past or how we got here.

I could speculate on the man that made me, but why bother; I am old now, and he is certainly dead. I did wonder when I was younger, and I came across another so like myself, but even then, I never pried. There was no point, I'd never know him. He was most likely a servant or slave, or perhaps a trader selling something exotic. He was certainly not Greek, that is clear from my complexion. I think he came from far away, Nubia or even further.

I hope he was her lover. I hope she had that at least. It's a nicer thought than the alternative, in many ways a nicer story than the fairy tale. In that version, they say that Zeus, king of the gods, lay with my mother whilst in the form of a swan. They say lay to make it more romantic I think, but we all know what it would be in this context. It was rape. As it always is in these stories. I hope my mother had better than that.

But I'm a realist, and I have my own experience to look back on.

I still have a brooch from my mother; it's small and plain, copper that has been etched with patterns. I found it in her box when I was very small. It is one of the stronger memories I have of Leda. I was hiding in a dark space, as I often did, perhaps behind a curtain or under something, and she came upon me while I was looking at that box. Rather than scolding me for touching her things, or being where I shouldn't, she smiled wide and whisked me up into her arms.

My mother had the most dazzling smile; she smiled with her whole face, eyes sparkling, mouth wide, she glowed. Made all the more lovely by its rarity.

She whisked me up and saw what I had. She took it from my hands and pinned it to my tunic. I remember she was speaking, but I cannot recall the words, just that her voice was pleasant, like a melody. Then she pulled me into her lap and rocked me gently as I continued to pull at the brooch. Wanting to see it.

If you looked carefully, you might mistake it for a swan.

I don't have a lot of memories of my mother. I remember her beautiful black hair and skin like cream; she was a classic beauty, though I looked very unlike her. She was pregnant most of the time when I was young, pushing out children only half of whom lived. She rarely left her rooms, or the palace itself; not to work the loom, to sit in the garden, or watch her living children. And when she did notice us, she would scowl or shout more often than hug us.

As a grown woman myself, I would think of her as melancholy, or something deeper I don't have words for. A doctor once told me about an affliction that in the East they called soul-sickness, when all the joys of life leave you; it was just after I lost my own Trojan sons, and he recommended fresh air, activity, and a new baby to heal. My soul-sickness receded, became duller and sometimes I'd forget about it completely, but I think my mother might have drowned in hers.

She died when I was 9, before I was old enough to really ask her the important questions. By that point, her hair was grey and wiry, and her skin looked like soured milk. In many ways, I think she might have died long before she was really gone.

Whoever my real father was, hero or villain, god or monster, my very human, earthly father was King Tyndareus of Sparta. You might be wondering what my relationship with him was like since I was so clearly not his daughter. Was he a kind-hearted man raising the offspring of only the gods knew who?

No.

Short, but true.

Why he didn't bash out my brains, even with the stories of my conception, I'll never know. He was a warrior, he was a politician, he was a scholar; he was ruthless and efficient in everything from managing his staff to military tactics. That's why so many kings and would-be kings wanted to marry his daughters; having Tyndareus as an ally was a sure victory. He was not given over to kindness. I might not know exactly why he kept me, but I know he had his reasons, he had a plan. I can take some comfort in whatever his plan was, I don't think it turned out as he expected.

As with my mother, I don't have that many memories of him, but for different reasons. He was busy; his place was not with the children and the women. And by the time I was born, my brothers were nearly men, he had heirs to train.

What I remember most is from after my mother died. I suppose that's when he finally noticed his children, the remaining girls, and realised we would need marriages soon. I think he might have looked at me properly for the first time only once she was gone.

By that point I was already getting stares and whispers. More than one boy had tried to kiss me, and even though I kept my head down it didn't stop people from approaching; people, men, seemed to bump into me regularly, or take the wrong turn. That was Paris' first gambit actually – "oh dear, I appear to be lost!"

Perhaps Tyndareus had finally heard the whispers, maybe someone had asked for my hand, whatever the reason, he looked at me. He looked the way I would start to get accustomed to being looked at, from toe to head, lips damp, eyes appraising. At that point, my body was still that of a child, but it was changing. I remember his damp fingers on my face as he pulled me towards him, examining me, opening my mouth to inspect my teeth like I was a slave.

He looked at me intensely and said 'smile'.

I did as he asked. I don't know what he was looking for, but he sighed, clearly disappointed. "Stop that. Don't smile, it ruins your face. Be serene, that works better for you."

I remember that specifically – be serene.

I think that was the first time someone had commented on me, boldly, to my face, rather than in hushed tones, behind their hands. It wouldn't be the last. For as beautiful as everyone said I was, everyone also seemed to have a lot to say about how beautiful I wasn't.

In hindsight, I took that last part to heart. I kept my face blank and calm; I didn't make waves. I was serene. It might have helped save my life, but I still feel anger and shame at the memory of it.

So not only was I not a daughter of the gods, but my parents were also hardly close to divine. But I hear you cry, what about the others? I had brothers and sisters, how do they fit into all this?

Well, if I'm not the daughter of divine intervention, then neither are they. I always find it funny that the stories about my birth have ended up scooping up the twins and Nest as well. I certainly was not a twin, and they were also not born in eggs. They were all clearly our father's children.

I was the fourth child, out of seven. Or seven that survived. There were the twins Castor and Pollux, Nest, then me, then Timandra, Philonoe, and Phoebe.

The babies, the last three girls, looked just like Nest. I suppose I should say, they looked like our mother, but by the time they were old enough for comparison she was gone, and Nest was there. I don't really remember them much. We were farther apart in ages, and I wonder even now if we were kept from each other – like dark skin might infect them. Philonoe was sent to be a virgin priestess, an acolyte of Artemis when she was very young; Phoebe died not long after mother; and Timandra was sent to her future husband's house just after my own marriage, despite her age. I barely remember them to be honest, and now, as I think on it, I feel so sad over that. I realise the songs and histories don't remember them either. How could they, compared to their older siblings? Those three little girls, lost to history and the greater story.

The twins, Castor and Pollux, the eldest, were almost identical to Tyndareus; broad with the same thinning hairline though one was more golden and the other darker. They were active boys when I was born and were practically men by the time I was old enough to understand a little of the world. They spent most of their time under the tutelage of their fighting masters and our father, learning how to be kings.

Nest had the exact same scowl as Tyndareus, though in all other respects she took after our mother, the same black hair though her skin was more the light bronze of the Mediterranean. Hopefully by now you've worked out that Nest is Clytemnestra. It was my name for her. She was the one who dubbed me Lena. No one else called us those names. At least not when we were children.

Nest and I were only together for 14 years, and yet she's the one I miss the most; my friend, my confidante. It's funny, so many seem to forget that we are sisters, married off to brothers. We stood on either side of the war at Troy, and neither of us got much out of it. No one seems to think that we two grew up together. We stood, maybe still stand, in each other's shadow; emblems of the failure of women.

Nest was only a year older than me; we were so close, and I can't imagine the world without her. Even now, I refuse to believe she isn't out there somewhere, although I know different. I said before I think I was kept away from the younger girls, but there was no way Nest would let me be kept from her.

We were also, so very different.

Nest would never wait to be spoken to; she always spoke first, spoke loudest, spoke longest. When we sat together at our looms, surrounded by other women, there was not a single topic she did not have an opinion on. She would even talk to Tyndareus like that.

She had her adventures; she swam nude in the lake, snuck wine from the cellar, eavesdropped on conversations. Once, she took our mother's most prized gown and cut it to her own size and style, and withstood mother dragging her to Tyndareus' side demanding punishment. He told her the dress fit Nest better. Occasionally I would join her in her madness, but mostly when she was sneaking and eavesdropping, when the adventure was safe, not on anything too bold.

When our mother died, I cried. I remember crying. And holding the babies who cried too. Nest didn't cry. Not around me anyway. She kicked things and stomped around and shouted. She would shout in our mother's room; she shouted some horrible things, and she swore she would never be like her.

Nest kept that promise.

She was the darling of Sparta, the right mixture of fierceness and virtue. I might have been considered the rare beauty, but Nest was classically beautiful; she glowed, and alongside that she could sew, hunt, and work the loom. A perfect Spartan princess.

And I was *her* favourite.

We'd talk into the night as we lay side-by-side, discussing our dreams and hopes and fears. I find myself chuckling at this; it sounds quite charming, but that's what sisters do. They either fight to the death or become the only friends they have. Oftentimes both.

If she had one fault, it's that she tended to let anything that went through her head come out of her mouth.

When at our looms once, some member of the household remarked, "you'll have to mind your tongue around your husband."

"I'll have a husband who likes my tongue as much as the rest of me" Nest replied with a smirk, and some appreciative tittering from the other ladies.

Someone else tutted and chimed in. "And what will you do when he doesn't, eh? When he likes another tongue instead, a softer, quieter one?"

"He shan't. And if he ever does..." Nest dragged her finger across her neck, killing her errant husband.

The woman chuckled. "Is that right? And then what? Do you think his men, his family will stand for that? Where would you go? What would you do? How would you live with such a curse on you?"

This turned Nest quiet, a rarity. She was thinking though. I could tell. She was pondering what that would mean.

"As I thought. Be more like this one." She nodded to me. "This one will be a proper wife. And she'll be happier for it."

There was a general murmuring of agreement. I remember thinking about responding, but what could I say? What response would possibly contribute to the conversation? Especially when it so reflected the mood of the land.

Of course, by proper wife she meant quiet and submissive. Serene. And that didn't make me anything like a proper wife.

Later, as we curled up, side by side, whispering about what happened throughout the day, Nest asked me about it, about husbands and the future and herself. I suppose the woman's comment had unsettled her.

"I don't think much about it" I replied. "I can read every thought on your face even before you say it out loud. You aren't that surprising".

"But that's because you know me" she contended.

"And you think your husband won't?"

She gave me a shrewd look. "You never really say what you think." She told me. "It's so hard to tell what's going on inside your head. You always win at any game because none of us can read you."

“And that’s good” I replied.

Nest shook her head, “But no one knows what you want. No one knows who you are.”

“And everyone knows what you want all the time!”

Nest nodded. “I think we need to consider a third option”.

“One that doesn’t involve murder!” I remember giggling.

I’m not sure we ever found that third option.

What are heroes like?

Apparently, we live in the age of heroes. Or that’s what the storytellers say, when they’re out singing their songs on the market street. I’m not sure what they really mean by that. Do they mean there are great men doing great deeds? Wars being fought? Or are there so many stories like mine, stories of gods and men that calling them heroes makes sense? We seem to be obsessed. Or at least, the Greeks do.

It’s the heroes the stories are all about; in theory they are about me or Troy, but really, they’re about the heroes. Ajax, Nestor, Agamemnon, and of course, the brightest of them all.

The great Achilles, the golden warrior who chose glory and death over life and obscurity. The Hero of Troy.

I never met him. At least, I do not remember meeting him. Or his lover and brother-in-arms Patroclus. Though I heard their names often enough. If either of them ever came to Sparta, they didn’t meet me. Tyndareus wouldn’t have liked that, and I don’t think Menelaus would have introduced us either. He wasn’t one for parties or introductions. I don’t even think Achilles came to our wedding, though I wouldn’t have noticed him there if he had. Funny again, how tied together our stories are, and yet we were never closer than a handful of miles.

Of course, I saw Achilles.

I saw him fight Paris, and I admit I had my fingers crossed at the outcome. But Paris turned and ran, as Paris did whenever anything went against him. I saw Achilles fight Hector. We all did, the entire House of Priam, standing on the high white walls of Troy; we watched him strike down Troy's favourite son, then desecrate his body screaming in… anger? Delight? Madness?

But I never met him, I didn't meet most of them. Though I saw them, light hitting their armour as they directed the phalanx across that desolate field. Achilles was golden, I suppose, in those moments. A golden speck. A flash of light against the burnt and blackened landscape, the legions behind him. They all were. That's how I think of most heroes now; bright but small. And dead.

There were some of the so-called heroes I was very close to, Menelaus and Paris, of course. And Odysseus. I suppose they were more than specks to me.

There were my brothers, Castor and Pollux. Their names sit in those lists of heroes, though they died long before Troy, a few years after mother.

They had an incredible sense of right and wrong, and loyalty. Especially to each other. They were together, always. In everything. Nest and I were close, but even we sometimes left each other's side. My brothers did not.

I recall Agamenon making some comment about that once. Menelaus shushed him. I didn't quite understand it then. I suppose whispers and gossip surround everyone, even the heroes.

Their deaths were awful. They had gone out, one in a chariot and one on a mare. The horses were found dragging the twins behind them. They were barely recognisable. No one knew exactly what happened. It looked like the horses had spooked, they'd lost control, and somehow both had been stamped and dragged to death.

I have never seen a man mourn as Tyndareus mourned his sons; his grief brought pain to everyone around him. A cloud settled over Sparta, obscuring everything, making it easier for clever men to play tricks. I know that grief myself, the loss of a child, of your children. I have felt it, and I know how it twists the world around you, dulls you to what else is going on, how it can let danger slip into your home.

By coincidence, Odysseus and a messenger from Mycenae arrived the next week.

It strikes me as amusing that Odysseus is the hero, the man, I think I have the best sense of. We only met three times, and yet, despite being married to Menelaus and Paris, seeing the rage of Agamemnon and the patience of Hector up close, its Odysseus that my mind strays to when I think of a hero.

Swift, cunning, sly. A man of whispers and shadows and schemes.

So, what was Odysseus to me?

He arranged my marriage. He unknowingly orchestrated my release from Troy. He inspired me to move on. All this, with only three meetings.

And, of course, he started the Trojan war. More or less.

So, what was I to him? That is harder. I was a pathway, a tool, a piece on the board he moved with an eye to his own future. Eventually, I was one of the few who understood him, who could speak with him on equal terms. But that is long after his first appearance in Sparta.

His appearance after my brothers' death was incredibly fortuitous. Sparta would need a new king, now the heir and the spare were both gone; Nest and I would need husbands; and my father would need counsel as he navigated this disturbing time. Who better than this bright young thing, blessed by Athena herself, or so they said.

To say he caused ripples would be an understatement. It was more like high waves that can drown an island. My father's old advisors were outraged that they were being ignored. That this upstart sat next to my father and shared his cup, whispering in his ear. It was such a scandal even I heard about it without having to hide behind doors or listen at windows.

We formally met once, though I saw him twice during that visit. I heard him more than saw him. Odysseus had the loudest laugh in the world; you could hear him booming throughout the palace. Sometimes, I could swear I heard it whilst in Troy.

But otherwise, he was quite plain; lean and taut, but neither tall nor short. His face was not remarkable, except for his nose. It had clearly been broken more than once. His looks didn't send the serving girls aflutter. It was only when he spoke that things changed. His voice was nice, deep and loose, and his way with words was unmatched. Or so they said. My experience with him didn't impress me that much. But he was clearly shrewd, collecting information, formulating plans, always thinking on both the short-term and long-term.

The first time I met him, he hadn't been at Sparta long. Tyndareus led him to Nest and I and introduced us, to an extent. Odysseus was helping him select husbands for us, and to do so he had to inspect the goods.

I remember his eyes narrowed, and he walked around us, then asked us to spin. I'm surprised he didn't check our teeth or run down our haunches.

I could feel his eyes lingering on me, even as I kept my gaze down. Remained serene.

I was surprised when he asked us questions. Very simple ones – what did we like to do? What did we think of the weather?

It was Nest who answered. I remained quiet, eyes downcast. Even when he tried to address me, I barely flicked my eyes up, and instead Nest prattled on about my weaving skills and my knowledge of plants. I remained silent.

As he left, Odysseus turned and stepped much closer than he should have. "You are a woman who knows proprietary." The smile that drew across his face was like a predator; it made me think of a lion. "That's good. That's easy." That sent a shiver down my spine, though I focussed on remaining still.

The second time I saw him, he didn't know he was being seen. Or at least, I don't think so. I also saw my second hero, Agamemnon. Not handsome exactly, but his face was full of emotion, anger and sadness, happiness, and love. He was full of life. I think that might be what drew Nest to him.

As the explorer, Nest knew all the nooks and crannies and passageways of the palace. She knew of a little used entrance by the guest rooms. It was her idea to sneak over to it and see if we could glean anything.

"He's going to marry one or both of us to one or both of them!" She declared. "I want to know what I'm getting. Don't you?"

"You don't know that. There are a lot of potential suitors" I remember suggesting, and it turns out I was half right. Nest just rolled her eyes at me.

"Of course, I want to know. I'm not an idiot. I want to be.... Prepared."

Nest snorted. "I cannot imagine anyone more unprepared."

She must have seen the look on my face. "Look, you're getting a husband no matter what. Why not get a peek at what men get up to first? Get an idea of what they think?"

She was right. We had very little engagement with men, and we both knew our parents had been ill-suited; wasn't I proof of that? So, I went with Nest on one of her adventures; the last one we had together as it turned out. We disrupted our sisters, poking and prodding them, so everyone in our rooms were focussed on soothing the babies, and then managed to creep silently along a dusty corridor, before we came to a lattice hiding a servant's entrance. The room on the other side was clearly little used; the things in it fine but worn.

We sat there for a while, legs cramping, but then we heard deep voices.

Some of their conversation I remember vividly, some only vaguely. I do remember the tone. That snide, chuckling tone that men often take with each other.

"What do you think?" Odysseus asked, there was a jug of wine ready and waiting for him, and he filled two cups. No water.

Agamemnon replied lightly, trying not to care "They're right about the youngest. I've never seen someone like her before. She is...."

"I know. But would you marry her?"

"Now that's the question. Would you?" Though I couldn't see his face, I could hear the smile, the leer, in his voice.

There was a pause as Odysseus considered his options.

"There's something about her. She's beautiful, but like a work of art. I'd want her to decorate my rooms, but I'm not sure I want to fuck her."

This I remember clearly. I remember the disgust and fear that rolled over me. I remember Nest's eyes, wide and bright and wet. We both realised there was only one way they could have this conversation; if they had already seen me, seen us. But we had never met Agamemnon, yet somehow... I still don't know how they did it; the same as us I suppose, a concealed place, some well-placed bribes.

Now I consider it, it really was not that hard to get around the Spartan palace undetected. A stronger lock on a door, fewer corrupted guards and perhaps I'm never writing this down. Perhaps Nest and I weren't as clever as we thought.

Agamemnon clearly considered Odysseus' answer before responding. "I wouldn't say that. I think I could manage to get my leg over. But she is quiet. And stiff. If I wanted my bed warmed by a statue, I could get that for a third of the price. The older one though…I like a woman with a spark".

Odysseus smiled. "You always did like spirit. More fun to break, eh? So, you want that one?"

"Not if you do. I could take the younger. Submissive can work for me" Agamemnon drained his cup and refilled it.

"I don't want either. Tyndareus won't let me any nearer the throne than I am now. He's still got some wiles left. I think he'll let you have the elder and Menelaus have the younger. Seems fair."

"And the crown?

"Menelaus of course. You'll get Mycenae. And I'll get whatever I can!" Odysseus' voice cracked slightly; like he was laughing but not with joy.

"Are you sure?"

"I've my eye on another one. Besides, I think there's a chance of trouble here." At that moment, Odysseus' eyes flicked towards the door we hid behind. There was no way he could see us, and yet it felt like our eyes met.

If Odysseus did know we were there, he showed no other sign. Agamemnon continued oblivious. "How? With the girls? With which one?"

"You know as well as I do that something's brewing. Words have been exchanged, and Priam is sniffing around places he shouldn't be. That son of his wants to be blooded, and it'll end in tears. And as for the girls. Both! The elder has a spark, but I think it's one that could light a fire. And the younger one. She's already been taken once. Given what they say about her, it's only a matter of time before something happens. There is something here, though. With Sparta and these two."

"What something?"

Odysseus looked back at the door. "Opportunity."

I remember being confused by his final word, but then we heard them moving and so hurried to get ourselves back to our rooms. If anyone saw us, they never said a word.

Of course, now I realise that Odysseus was already putting pieces on his game board. I didn't know what was happening around the world, but he did. And he saw how the die might fall and was positioning himself as well as everyone else. He saw 'opportunity'. I wonder how much I figured into that opportunity then. And whether he really knew what it would lead to?

The final time I saw Odysseus, that was exactly what we spoke about. About his actions and plans, was it all worth it? We were sitting on a beach overlooking the ocean, neither of us young nor pristine any longer. I remember he told me that it was worth it. It had to be. But I think I'll save that conversation for later in the story.

Menelaus

It's time to talk about my poor Menelaus.

Yes, I call him that. He was mine, and he was poor. I didn't feel sympathy for him during our marriage, but from the moment I left I have felt almost nothing but that. I'm not sure if that makes me a good person or not.

He wasn't perfect, but he wasn't bad either. As husbands go, as Kings go, he was good enough. And my life in Sparta, those 10 years as his wife, were perfectly fine.

He tends to fade away compared to the other men in the story. Agamemnon is handsome and war-hungry; Odysseus is clever and swift; Achilles is bold and strong. And Menelaus is…

What is he?

A cuckold? A weak man? A failure?

He wasn't any of those things.

It happened much as Odysseus said it would. Tyndareus decided that I should go to Menelaus, and he would be king of Sparta, and that Nest would go to his brother in Mycenae. Two sisters for two brothers. People always like that idea.

Nest was ecstatic. She knew exactly what she would be as a Queen. She would be good and regal and have an heir within the year. She'd already seen Agamemnon and she liked what she saw.

I was more hesitant. I was glad I wasn't going to one of the men who'd been hanging around, who lurked in shadows around Tyndareus, making comments about my suitability. But I didn't know anything about Menelaus. I was apprehensive; worried about how I felt, if he would like me, all the usual things girls in my position worry about.

I was also worried about those words I'd heard Odysseus say – cold, like a statue. They niggled at me, especially at night. I'd tried to explain it to Nest when we returned to our room, but it's the one time I don't think she really understood.

As soon as we'd gotten back, she'd started gushing, convincing herself she was already in love. And why not? She was 15 and had no choice, why not convince yourself you feel it.

"And you're going to be with his brother. We'll be sisters twice over. I'm sure his brother is as good a match as he is. And you don't have to marry Odysseus!"

"How did they know about us? They spoke like they'd seen us. And what did he mean? About there being an opportunity with us?" I asked carefully. I wasn't sure Nest had picked up on that.

Of course, I could also be remembering this all wrong.

"I'm sure he just meant you'd be a good choice for Agamemnon's brother. And I'm the perfect choice for Agamemnon" She gave me a mischievous smile. "Ignore the other things he said. You know you are beautiful and desired. Everyone says so."

The falter in her voice, the look in her eye, the way she blushed, for a moment I wondered if she was jealous. It was the only time I wondered what she saw in me, and whether there was something other than love buried in her.

All I felt was cold. She'd ignored the first part of my question; maybe she'd already met Agamemnon in person, it was the sort of thing she would do. But there was something more. Nest had spoken more than once about feeling desire, this tingle as she called it. I had awoken to strange noises coming from her bed. Odysseus had dismissed me as a potential wife because he viewed me as cold – isn't that how I was supposed to be? He'd praised my calmness to my face, Tyndareus told me to be serene. I felt confused and wrong.

"Nest, what if he's right and I'm like a statue?" I asked her.

"How? What do you mean?"

"I just…that…what you talk about, that feeling, that… tingle. I've never felt it. What if he's right, and I'm like stone? What if I'm not right inside?" Just like I'm different on the outside, I thought; maybe there's something in my blood that means I'm broken.

I spoke slowly. I wanted her to understand, and to listen, and I both wanted to say it and didn't. I knew I was blushing; this was intimate, private, even between sisters. Even now it's hard to write, though so much time has passed, and I understand myself so much better.

Nest folded me into her arms. "Don't fret Lena. It doesn't mean anything. You hardly talk to any men, and you haven't met your husband yet. I'm sure once you do, it'll come. And you'll be so happy."

Her confidence gave me confidence. I was hopeful she would be right for such a long time.

That feeling never came though. Not with Menelaus, Paris, or even by myself. It caused me a lot of pain when I was younger, not feeling that desire. I want to emphasise that I loved my children, and I understand that without sex they wouldn't be here. But still, I didn't feel the need for it, I still don't.

How ironic right? The most beautiful woman in the world doesn't like having sex. It does almost feel like a tragedy. Except otherwise I wouldn't be where I am now, I wouldn't have Entef, I wouldn't be happy in my old age.

More than one wise woman or priestess told me it was natural; women feeling that desire, that tingle as Nest called it, was unnatural and masculine, and this meant I was more woman than those others. But that seemed wrong too. It didn't fit with the language, the ideas, that surrounded me.

I still wanted to be held though, touched, cuddled, but at that age I didn't understand it, and I could never articulate it. I spent a long time starved of touch and tenderness because of it.

I find it funny now, that I spent so much time worrying about it. But then again, the few men who met me always ran their eyes over my body and made it clear what they wanted to do. Now those same men wouldn't look at me twice. Though experience suggests they'd still pounce, if they could get away with it; they just wouldn't look at me. Perhaps I was cursed by Aphrodite! But I no longer feel like I must be broken. I feel at peace with myself.

I didn't meet Menelaus until the wedding.

Nest and I were married at the same time. I honestly don't remember much about that day. It was such a blur.

I remember the anxiety sitting like ice in my stomach. I remember Nest pushing a cup of wine into my hands to help me calm down, even though she was the one who wouldn't stop – moving, speaking, tapping her feet, adjusting her clothes.

There were also remarks from the Mycenaean ladies who joined us. I suppose they'd spoken to other people at the palace, or rumours were spreading outside of Sparta well before this. I'd only ever been outside the palace once, and no one would have spoken to them in my hearing, or Tyndareus'. They commented on my hair and skin, on my body, on my lustfulness and my fertility. They seemed especially enraptured by my hair; so different, so special. I'd have had to be deaf not to hear the edge in their voices, even as they reached out to caress it.

They weren't the first to make such comments, though I suppose at Sparta people had gotten used to me. But these words would follow me for the next twenty years or more. How different I looked, my hair, my skin, my eyes, and how they could be adjusted. I always just nodded, let them do what they wanted. Now there's very little to do anything with, and no one troubles me. But then…

As I write this, I realise how the background of my life is filled with the soft wind of whispers; of talk hidden behind hands and soft tones. It's always been there. And what did I do about it?

What could I do?

I sat in silence. I let everyone fuss around me, and I waited to be ready. I knew I needed to be perfect; those ladies proved it. I was serene.

I first saw Menelaus at the ceremony. I'm sorry to say that my first thought was that he was old. He was older than his brother, by at least five years. His face was lined, and his hair had a tinge of silver at the temples. His beard was still thick and dark though, and he had a powerful frame.

In the stories they tell now, they say that Menelaus is the younger son. It makes sense, he didn't take the throne of Mycenae, and perhaps it makes him seem weaker, more likely to lose a wife. Though he was a soldier, a conqueror, a king just as much as his brother, if not better suited to it.

But he was the elder, and it showed, in his features, his face, and his bearing.

I remember he was gentle when he took my hand, his smile was soft, and he whispered to me to be calm. That made me smile ever so slightly. He would soon learn I was calm. Always.

It was the marriage feast that everyone remembers though. It's what started it. That night, those words, its where the seeds of Troy's destruction were sown.

I remember it being loud. I was sitting with Menelaus, his hand was still in mine, and I was nibbling at the food, sipping at my cup. I was still veiled, though Nest's was thrown off, completely inappropriate, and she was laughing along with Agamemnon. They seemed to be touching each other a lot.

Then the speeches. There must always be speeches at these things.

When Odysseus stood up, and the whole room fell silent. That's partly how I know it was so loud because that silence was deafening.

I suppose he saw this as an opportunity. He must have planned out what he would say, timed it so the guests were sober enough to remember it, but drunk enough to be roused by what he said.

I don't recall his speech exactly, but I can tell you generally. Besides, isn't this what writers of history do? Write the words as they remember them, even if they're wrong? And this moment was history.

Odysseus' voice was strong and expressive. I didn't need to see his face to know what was written there as he spoke.

"Welcome all and join me in giving the greatest blessings to the new couples. May you be fruitful and successful, may you live long, and may the gods look down fondly upon you. Of course, in at least one case here, that must be assured."

There was laughter at the comment, some mild tittering that still showed how uncomfortable everyone was. That would change.

"I will be looking to my good friends for advice in their marital felicity, as I will be joining that state soon. I am delighted to let all gathered here know that I have accepted the hand of King Icarus' daughter, Penelope of Ithaca. So, I will be cousin-in-marriage to my dear friends. I hope to see all of you at that celebration, though I know that my company is not nearly as elevated as that of the grooms here."

That caused more general murmuring, a clear note of surprise at this announcement. Not to mention the way it was announced, as though Odysseus was the prize catch. You could almost feel what everyone was thinking – this nobody has charmed his way into Ithaca. You could also feel the interest, the increase in attention; this nobody was about to become somebody, and his words could be important.

"And although I know that my Penelope is beautiful and kind, as is Clytemnestra, the wife of my good friend here, I am not a fool. And no one else in this room is either. There is one lady who I know men lust after. Who I know could bring down the wrath of the gods if she is unhappy. Who is more than a woman. Dearest Helena, wife of Menelaus, would you unveil yourself please?"

I remember the subtle gasp that went up. I remember Menelaus squeezing my hand in reassurance. I suppose he was in on this gambit. I didn't really understand. I looked to Tyndareus, but he was staring straight ahead, gaze lost somewhere above the door.

I moved like I was under water. Slowly. Too slowly it seemed. It was Agamemnon who ripped the veil from my face.

The room was frozen. I kept my eyes cast down. I didn't want to see them looking at me. I wanted to be humble and serene and perfect. But I could feel it. I could feel those eyes over my body, touching, roaming, judging. I could feel the shift in the room, through the haze of fire and wine and food, something else entering. Call it lust or want, it was like a blanket cast across the crowd, smothering it.

I want you to understand something. I had been told I was beautiful. I had heard I was of another world. I knew I was different; my skin and hair did not match my siblings, and there were constant whispers that my complexion was closer to a slave than a princess. But never until that moment had I really thought that that could mean something, could impact something, larger than myself. I had no idea what Odysseus was going to say next, but I knew he would be using me as a part of a bigger game.

"When looking upon such a face, who could deny that this is a daughter of the gods. Who, when observing this figure, could not want to touch it. Who could not wish to listen to the voice that comes from those lips.

But she is now a wife. The wife of our comrade. Our brother. She will be the mother of his children and the queen of his land and the woman in his bed. And she will be his forever.

I want all of you to join me in taking a vow. That none of us will ever ruin this home. That none of us will ever try to take this queen. And if any do, that we shall rise to defend our brother, our friend, and rescue his wife from her captors."

I was breathing heavily. Quickly. Too quickly. I couldn't slow down. I could feel my heart pounding, my head was swimming, and I felt the room pressing down around me. I fell rather than sat back down, pulling the ripped pieces of my veil over my face, trying to cover myself. It was then I realised my face was wet. I'd started crying.

Men were shouting oaths, cheering, wine was flowing, and it felt like the room was on a knife edge, though I didn't know what falling would mean.

Menelaus tried to take my hand again, but I pushed him away, hard. He grabbed my hand anyway, harder. I was still trying to get control of my breath.

I glanced down the table. Nest looked horrified and was saying something to Agamemnon; I think that was their first fight. Starting as they meant to go on.

And Tyndareus...he was gone. He must have realised in that moment, as we all did, that Odysseus was playing a complex and dangerous game, and we were right in the middle of it.

Odysseus used my marriage to bind the Greeks together in the event of my disappearance. Agamemnon and Menelaus were part of it. I don't know where this idea came from. Maybe they knew my past, what had already happened. Maybe they just took a chance. If so, it was a calculation that worked.

Something else came from that night though. The rumours about me grew, turned from rumours to stories to fact. I know there had been some before, and some of them had made their way outside the palace, so that a few might believe them. But it hadn't been like this, with the good and great of the world hearing these words.

I wonder what those men saw. When my veil was torn away, and my face put on display. Did they look at me and think me beautiful? Or did they look at me through their wine-laced gaze and hear Odysseus say I was beautiful, that I was the daughter of a god, and decided it must be true?

Does it even matter?

Either way, it had very little to do with me. I think that was the night that created Helen of Troy.

I think I know what next question you would ask me – what of the wedding night?

We can't help it. Sex occupies so many minds, and you cannot help but wonder about mine. Especially given what you've already heard of my story. What happened that night? How did I feel? Did I fall in love with Menelaus there?

Like so many women before and since, I didn't choose to be in Menelaus' bed, but I accepted that was my role. I had expected it, even wanted to get married. It was the way of the world. Consent without desire. It sums up so much now I think on it, so much of my life. I want you to understand that love and desire are different to acceptance and expectation. It was this with Menelaus, just as it would be with Paris later.

That night we went to my new room, one for the lady of the palace, no longer a child. It smelt of flowers and incense. I was nervous, still overcome by what had happened. Sounds silly to say, maybe it seems obvious, but I was nervous, and it showed. I was shaking slightly, even though the room was warm, and the bed was soft.

I'm not sure what I thought Menelaus would do first. I did not expect him to hug me.

It was not erotic or sensual. It was a full-bodied embrace. It calmed me. He always smelt good; deep and spicy. It felt nice to be wrapped up in someone's arms.

We stood like that for a while.

When we broke apart, he led me to my bed, and we sat down.

"Hello Helena. I am Menelaus. It's nice to meet you" he said in his deep voice.

I nodded and said hello back.

"I want to be honest. I do not know what you are thinking. I for one, am pleased to have you as my wife. And I'm pleased to be the next king of Sparta. I want us to be friends. I want us to have children. I want us to rule in peace. And I want us to be honest with each other. Do you understand?"

When I nodded again, he smiled. "You are lovely Helena."

He gently placed his hands on my head, on my hair.

"So lovely"

He light ran his fingers down my arm, pulling at my dress.

"So lovely"

His hand cupped my bared breast.

"So lovely" he repeated each time a new piece of me was revealed.

He was saying it more to himself than complimenting me. But he was soft and slow and gentle. There was some pain, that first time, but I was more sore than anything.

He lay next to me and slept afterwards, and I lay next to him awake. I wasn't thinking about anything. I distinctly remember not thinking or trying not to. Eventually my mind was disturbed by other noises. It took me a while to realise it was Nest. There were screams and shouts and grunts and groans.

I giggled to myself and woke up Menelaus. He heard them too and smiled at me.

I think that's how it could have been between us forever.

Nest's leaving was, up to that point, the greatest tragedy of my life. That sounds terrible, when I'd already lost my mother and brothers, but they did not compare to Nest. She only stayed a couple of weeks after the wedding, Agamemnon wanted to get home.

We stood together shaking and crying as we said goodbye. Agamemnon huffed as he waited for us to be done, mumbling about the tide, while Menelaus stood good naturedly shrugging.

We promised to write, to send messages and gifts. But she was going further than we realised and messages get lost.

I remember touching her arm and she flinched. She had already started getting bruises, and the only thing that stopped me from commenting was that Agamemnon appeared to be getting the same number.

When Nest walked out of the palace, I felt a void open. That void has never fully closed. Not when my children were born, and not now, as I find myself being happy.

We never met again.

It was only a year later that Tyndareus died.

Big life events always seem to happen at the same time. Within the space of a year I was married, I lost Nest, and Tyndareus left us. And there were all the happenings in between.

There was a great show of mourning; wailing could be heard throughout the palace, and everyone was careful to be sombre. The tomb was already built, so it was easy to say goodbye and wish him luck in the underworld.

A few kings and dignitaries came, though not as many as at my wedding. The one that stands out is Hector; that was my first experience of Troy. He was sent to pay his respects on behalf of his father. As I stood veiled, he came over and gently kissed my hand and offered his condolences. He was soft spoken, with kind eyes that crinkled, but his hand was strong and callused. I don't think I really took him in then, and when I try to picture him, I can only conjure up the man 15 years later. I must try hard not to see the ripped, ragged, decomposing body left on the steps of Troy.

My emotions were muddled then; Tyndareus had been a constant, but he hadn't been my father. It was a shock to lose him, to no longer have him around. But it was a relief as well. Leaving me alone, making Menelaus king.

Odysseus also came back; risky given he was only just married to Penelope. He didn't spend much time in open mourning though. He grabbed Menelaus as soon as he arrived, and they were locked in a room for hours. He even skipped the feast. No doubt forming more plans. Grasping more opportunities

Nest wasn't able to come; she was pregnant, and it was far too dangerous. She wrote me a lovely note about it.

That is when my life with Menelaus really began.

It was quiet in many ways. Menelaus typically spent the day with his men, ruling, talking, hunting, and would visit me at night.

I never got that desire, but it wasn't unpleasant. For the first few months he visited me every night, even when I bled. Every time I disrobed, he would stroke me and call me lovely. He would tell me where to lie, or sit, or kneel, where to place my hands, my mouth, my legs, and I would. It was easy to do. And he enjoyed it. I wanted to be a dutiful wife. Serene in all things.

I did enjoy talking to him afterwards. He always stayed for a time; continuing to stroke and caress and cuddle. I think he knew I liked that part the best. As we lay together, I would ask him questions about the outside world. It felt safe to ask then, safer than it had been before. And he would answer, happy to show off his travels, his knowledge, his experience.

So, what to say about him?

Of course, he was a warrior. How could any king of Sparta not be?

People forget that about Menelaus. He was a warrior long before he was a king. Long before any of those other heroes were heroes. He had already fought Priam once on the battlefield. And won.

He had scars. He had a small one along his brow, that curved down his face and drove a trough through his beard. A deep triangle on his thigh from an arrow. And a long vivid one down the length of his arm. His knuckles were littered with them.

Once, whilst we lay in bed, I asked him about them. He smiled sweetly.

"You don't need to know about the wars of the world" he whispered.

I shook my head, "I want to know about your wars".

He had sighed and smiled and continued. "Which one first?"

I lightly touched his leg.

"Ah, the arrow. That came when I was a much younger man. During the siege of Mycenae. When my brother and I were fighting our way through the gates to get back our city, our birthright. Your father was there, sitting high on a horse, watching, shouting orders. Once we broke through the walls, the archers turned their bows inwards, and I was struck. I fell. Agamemnon came to me, but I urged him on."

He paused then. Unsure of whether he should say the next words.

"It took me a moment, but I was able to tie up the wound and go after him. That's how I found him. Covered in blood sitting on the throne with our uncle, Thyestes, dead at his feet. The look on his face...Maybe he wanted it more. He was so young when we left, he barely knew our father. But still..."

"Is that why you came here instead?"

Menelaus was the older son. By rights, Mycenae was his. Everyone knew he had said his brother could have the throne as he had gotten to it first. Then again, everyone also knew that Thyestes had run away rather than fight. People, I have learned, don't know anything.

"It wasn't my father's throne. It was his now. And...there was something about that image. Glorious Agamemnon, covered in blood. It was right and wrong".

Menelaus drifted off for a moment.

He came back when I touched his arm. That scar was much redder, though by the end of our marriage it would fade.

“This was two years ago. A small skirmish along Illium. Pirates! Or so Priam said. It’s amazing how many pirates who sound like Trojans end up taking Greek ships! I ended up facing a beast of a man. He was big and strong, but I was faster. Not fast enough to dodge his blade entirely, but still. When he came down, the entire ship shook”.

He reached around me shaking the bed, causing me to giggle and shriek.

Finally, we came to his brow.

He looked sheepish. That’s not an expression you often hear about heroes of legend having, but rest assured, they have reasons to be sheepish just like the rest of us. “This is from when I was younger. A training accident. A wooden sword. You should have seen the other guy. Not a scratch on him!”

I giggled again, and Menelaus laughed, and we lay there for a while. Until he bid me goodnight and left. I curled up to sleep, feeling…content.

I suppose that’s how Menelaus made me feel. Content. Fine.

Menelaus was a good ruler. He had the pedigree of a king, the decisiveness of the battlefield, and the calm of a statesman. He always knew the path he wanted to take, and if there was any hesitancy, he had his advisors. Most especially his brother; letters flew between them like they had wings. When I think of the man he was then, and the man he became, it fills me with sadness. Not guilt, I do not think it was me who moulded him into something different. But sadness that what happened could rend such a change.

The only real change in him in our years together was in relation to war; he didn't go on campaign anymore. He was happy to let younger men fight, and to rule from the throne. I know this caused anger in some corners, and he would occasionally comment about this at night. It seemed very little would push Menelaus from his home now he was settled.

He remained strong at home too. In the bedroom, when he came by, he would still tell me what he wanted. Though. over time, it became clear he didn't necessarily want me.

I never loved Menelaus, not like that, though I had, still have, affection for him. I thought we were happy, and I was being a good wife, doing what I was supposed to do. Which is why it still hurt when he started his affair.

The first one is most notorious; it bore one of his sons. I say first, but I really mean the first I knew about. I'm sure there were other women before, in between, but this one lasted long enough for me to hear about it.

It happened slowly. First, he stopped caressing me and talking after sex, then he stopped telling me how lovely I was or giving instructions, and then he stopped coming as often, and then he didn't come at all.

More whispers. But now they were accompanied by pitying looks and rooms falling silent when I entered.

For my part, I noticed his absence. I wasn't sad about the sex, but I knew I couldn't have a baby without it. I missed the feeling of being close to someone. I didn't have many people to talk to, even if my conversations with Menelaus were one-sided.

It didn't take long for me to realise what was going on, as sheltered as I was, I knew. But it still hurt, like a thorn into my heart. When the realisation came, I felt sick. I couldn't leave my room for days as I thought of the shame of what people would say. What they had been saying. I was only 15.

Eventually, I emerged, and I had a plan. I remember I sat at my loom, and the other women around me, sewing and talking and laughing. I knew this was my moment.

"Who is she?" My back was to them. It became quiet, and I knew they were glancing at each other, deciding what to say. "Who is she?" I repeated.

"There's no need…" came a small voice. I felt a spark of anger and asked again, harsher 'Who is she?"

There was an audible sigh, and then an older voice spoke up. I'll always appreciate that no one asked me who I was talking about.

"A girl. A slave girl. From the kitchen. She serves in the hall sometimes."

That made sense to me. A beautiful girl who brought wine and could not refuse; how could any man resist?

"Her name?" I asked.

This time the quiet was different. Some of them certainly did not know, but some did. I waited the silence out. One of the plus sides of being serene; you can wait out anybody.

"Nysa" came a younger voice than before.

“Let’s call for some wine and have Nysa serve us” I spun round and looked at the slave in the corner, who bowed and quickly ran from the room.

The tension began to rise as we sat there. I could feel my face was of stone. There was music being played, and some of the women tried to talk again, but it was no use.

We sat and waited for our wine to be delivered.

Of course, someone must have warned the girl what had happened. When a figure appeared at the door, there was a stiffness in her shoulders, and a wariness in her body; like a deer who senses the hunter.

She came in with a large jug, eyes down. She slowly moved to place the jug somewhere. I held out my cup to her. She had no choice but to come over.

I wanted to study her.

My initial reaction was ‘this?! This is what he prefers instead of me?! He goes to this instead of his wife, his queen.’

Perhaps all the talk had finally gone to my head, and I believed I was irreproachable; the most beautiful, the desire of every man. But even then, I think I knew that looks aren’t everything between two people.

She was older than me, by at least 10 years, though that only made her 25; an adult to me then, and a baby to me now. She had that starved leanness slaves often have – too much work and too little food. Her hair was pulled back, but was thick and coarse, her eyes were dark brown, and she had a small scar on her lip. I know she was a lovely looking woman; normal perhaps, but lovely.

Yet, seeing her was a jolt. That this was who he wanted instead of me.

I realised she was shaking as she poured, the wine was in danger of spilling. I reached out and held her wrist. She glanced up at me then, and there was such fear there. I'm not sure anyone had ever looked at me in fear before. It struck me in a way I can't describe. I felt shame wash over me. I'd like to say I learnt something from that experience, but not much, I was still so young, and any lessons would come later.

"Set it down and you can leave" was all I said. And she rushed out.

It's amazing how many types of silence exist, and how many echoed through that room that afternoon. This one was strained in a new way. Everyone waiting for my reaction.

I maintained my composure and sipped my wine. Then I turned back to the loom.

Slowly the music and talking resumed, almost like nothing had happened.

Once I had drained my wine, I slipped away complaining of a headache. But just as Nest and I did so long ago, I paused to listen, hidden behind a lattice door, and sure enough, they soon started talking about me.

Comments along the lines of how bold I was, how scandalous it was, how different we were as women, how could anyone want that when they had a woman that looked like me?!

Those I had been expecting, but two other comments were a surprise.

“Perhaps she’ll have an affair of her own? Embarrass him as he’s embarrassed her,” Someone said.

“The apple doesn’t fall far from the tree after all. And the blood that must be in her, she must be ready for anyone.” Coarse laughter filled the air.

“So long as she doesn’t come after my husband”.

“I’ve heard Lyander talk of her. Apparently, there are bets going as to who can slip between those thighs first.”

“She’s best kept away from the men. For her good as much as theirs.”

“But why would he move on though? And so soon? With no baby?”

“Perhaps she’s frigid? What man wants to lie with a cold fish”?

More cackling.

I felt that sick feeling wash over me again. Their words were so reminiscent of those I’d heard before, and the ones that ran through my head at night. The tears spilled, and I really did return to my room ill.

Menelaus visited me that night. I should have been ready, should have known word would reach him.

I was lying on the bed staring up at the ceiling. I felt his presence before I saw him. I could feel his glower.

He didn’t say anything, but he undressed and sat on the bed, his back to me.

He made no noise as he rolled on top of me and grabbed my throat. I could feel my pulse beating against his hand. When our eyes met, I could see the anger in him, the power. I could feel his fingers itching to squeeze. But he didn't. Maybe because he saw his anger reflected back at him. It was only a moment, but I saw the warrior, the madman, that lived inside my husband.

He removed his hand, then said, "on your front".

He didn't stay to talk.

Nysa bore Menelaus' first son, Megapenthes, who would eventually follow his father to Troy. I sent clothing and toys when he was born. I couldn't be angry at her, or at a child. This is the way of the world. And Menelaus too was kind to them, even after he'd put Nysa aside.

It became a ritual of mine. When I realised that he had another woman, I would call her to me. It was easiest with slaves and servants, it was harder with other women, but few would refuse me outright. Everyone began to know it was coming, and I would feel the anticipation in the air, a flutter through the women around me as I appeared in my best dress, my finest jewels, and called a name to bring me wine or to talk to me.

If there was a child, I'd always send gifts.

Menelaus never said or did anything else after the first time.

I'm not sure I ever felt as powerful as a Queen as in those moments.

I realise that I've told you Menelaus was a kind man, then told you how he betrayed me, even hurt me. Perhaps it's my memory playing tricks again. Or its just knowing that each of us has so many parts, they come to the surface as they will.

My own first child came less than a year after Menelaus' first. It pains me to think she was created in anger, but what can be done about that.

Many people are confused about my children, so I'll put that straight right now. I had four; one girl and one boy with Menelaus and two boys fathered by Paris. Any others belonged to somebody else.

Hermione was the easiest; I was young then, only 16. She was small but strong. Menelaus was pleased, though I could tell he was disappointed it wasn't a boy.

I was besotted. She became my world. I would neglect my other work just to watch her. She could be with me as much as I wanted, and I strapped her to myself like the peasant women did and carted her with me.

Eventually, Menelaus had to tell me to stop. It wasn't long after he'd resumed coming to my bed. It was afterwards. He was stroking my back; he'd asked me to lie on my stomach. It was still swollen, and he didn't wish to see that, but you couldn't really tell from the back. He leaned over to whisper in my ear, "You need to leave the baby with the nurse. You cannot take her everywhere."

I smiled up at him. "But I want to. I just…want to be with her. I want to see her face when she sees the world".

I had spoken at a normal volume, but Menelaus sighed and continued to whisper, "Your maternal instincts do you credit, and it is understandable given your past. But you must leave her with her nurse".

I went to protest, but he pinched me and hissed, "No wife of mine will cart her baby like a common whore. You will leave her with her nurse, and you will focus your energies on running my house. I don't expect to need to tell you again".

I nodded, ducking my head down to hide my tears. Menelaus continued to stroke my back, my arm, avoiding my stomach.

Hermione looked like me when she was younger; lighter and her eyes were brown, but otherwise I could see she was my daughter. I hear stories that say she has a strong mind; she was certainly outspoken as a child. I hope with all my heart that that is true.

The boys were harder.

Aethiolas was born a few years before I left Sparta; he was so round, like a ball, and such a happy thing. Menelaus was delighted to have another son, a proper heir. He didn't show it in praise or any of those ways you might expect. But I could see it, in the way his gaze fell on him, the way he would stumble into the nursery constantly, and the little trinkets left for both of us.

Menelaus loved his children, whoever their mother was, whatever caused their existence, he loved and cared for all of them.

The only real tragedy in our lives were the lost children. I had two between Hermione and Aethiolas, one died in my womb, and one lived only a few days. Menelaus held me whilst I screamed out my grief and helped me regain my strength. But he also left me to see to his own needs; he had more than one bastard while I cried over our lost children.

I wonder what Hermione and Aethiolas thought of me? Or think of me now. Hermione spent time with me, 8 years together, she was a little person when I left. But Aethiolas; he wouldn't remember me. I wonder what they were told? What they thought? Did they think I abandoned them?

Though I suppose I did; willing or not, I left my children.

And what of the Helena that returned? But that's a story for later.

No one talks about my Trojan children. I don't talk about them. I don't think I can.

Aganus and Bunomus were born at Troy. They pass through my thoughts every day but stopping to let them in…That is still hard.

They died. They were killed by war. It was awful.

They were so young.

It never goes away those feelings – grief, guilt, anger. I remember overhearing one of the ladies of Troy whisper it was my punishment from the gods. As though being in Troy wasn't some sort of punishment enough. I don't think I have ever truly lost my temper as I did then. I was told her eye healed, though she had a scar.

Good. I hope she is still alive. That she is bound as a slave to a Greek family and every time she sees or touches her face, she finds that scar and thinks of Helena of Troy and her dead children.

Maybe I can talk about them more later. Maybe.

I loved my children, but I lost them all, one way or another.

That's what it was like for nearly ten years.

I spent my days much as I had before, though now I was more elevated. I ran the household. I entertained the wives of important men, spent time at my loom, drinking wine, and even gossiping on occasion. More than one woman commented on how demure I was; I'm still not sure if they meant it as a compliment. Women are supposed to be demure, aren't they? And yet, it still has the sting of an insult.

I realise as I write this that I haven't mentioned the other women much. I was surrounded by them, but there is no one I can pull out as a friend. Perhaps I should have tried harder. I was young and became a queen to women who had always had authority over me, so it was difficult to assert this position. But I should have tried, especially as their daughters and newcomers joined us.

I never did though. I kept myself separate. That probably didn't help the whispers; if you don't let people know you, they'll fill in the blanks themselves. Nest had told me you could never tell what I wanted. Perhaps if I'd tried harder, if I'd made friends with those women, none of this would have happened? I would have been protected in another way.

The truth is, I've only ever really had two strong female friends. I have never taken the chance to make more. And why? Maybe because of my own vanity, maybe because of theirs. In Troy it was because I was the enemy and the reason for fighting, but in Sparta? I just found I couldn't, and those other women didn't try to befriend me either.

I could also act contrary. I know I did things those women did not like, they thought proud or cruel. Like my insistence on meeting Menelaus' women face-to-face. Or like when I had all the shiny surfaces removed from my quarters, and then the ladies' rooms. I'd never liked them, I'd always avoided them, and now I could do what I wanted with them. Perhaps that tied into the perception of how demure I was? Perhaps they thought I was expressing a perverse form of vanity? Perhaps all those women are now dead and gone and it never mattered what they thought, and no one will remember them at all? Except me, who sits here and wonders.

And so, I sat on my throne, resplendent in my beauty and power. Alone.

I suppose that's my bitterness coming through. Even as I tell you how happy I was, how much I understand their view now, I still have this streak of black that bubbles up. Why is that?

It was during those first few years of marriage that I finally discovered something for myself. Yes, I had my daughter, and I love her. And I had my duties. But I had never really loved a thing, had something I did for my pleasure rather than for praise. And I finally found it.

Just as Menelaus decreed, I could no longer take Hermione everywhere with me, so I decided to try something new; to fill the time I had spent with her. I had always loved the gardens, I had spent so much time in them, as had my mother when she could, so I turned to them.

I was always better at indoor pursuits. They say Penelope was great at the loom, a true talent, but I pride myself on my own skills too. I started to incorporate the plants I saw into my sewing, and to my surprise, they seemed to appeal to the women at the palace. Or they pretended to like them…I'm not sure. You might be thinking, if I was so great at needlework, why not embrace that as something to love. I did enjoy that, but it was expected, something I would aways have to do. But the gardens were something I could choose to do.

I began by talking to the gardeners now and then. I asked to see what they were doing, and slowly I built up my knowledge and started doing more. They wouldn't let me near the kitchen gardens at first, so I started with flowers and borders, but eventually they relented. I don't want you to think I became an expert, or that my life was consumed by the earth, but it was something to enjoy for its own sake.

When we look back at the past we see the paths, the twists and turns, the patterns; life can seem so inevitable when we're living it, but looking back we see how much was chance. A random decision can have as much impact as a long-considered proposal. If I had not decided to go into those gardens, to talk to those gardeners, to plunge my hands into that dark earth, would I be telling this story?

I suppose it doesn't much matter, as I am telling it. And so, I filled my days with dirt and thread; learning about plants, cultivating them, and sitting at my loom, sewing what needed to be sewn.

It seemed like this is how I would live out the rest of my life. Not unhappy. Not spoilt. Not with an angry and cruel husband. Not surrounded by friends. Not without purpose and love and light.

We lived as husband and wife, as king and queen. We did our duty. After Nysa, Menelaus returned to me, with the same affection as before, and we talked and laughed, and he told me stories of the world and I told him stories of our daughter and my garden.

He had other women, though I was better prepared for them and took those times to enjoy being by myself. To be able to dig my hands into the earth and not have to worry about being presentable.

Occasionally, he asked questions about me. He would ask about my day and my gardens and my loom.

Not a bad life, all told.

But that's not how the story ends.

Abductions

I worry that if I don't get to the good stuff soon, you'll abandon the story. So, I thought I should answer what I think to be one of your other burning questions – about Paris and the night we left for Troy.

The canny amongst you will notice that this title is a plural. This is because I have been abducted more than once. Three times in all.

The first time, I was just a baby, but Nest has told me the tale many times, so I give it to you in her words.

"One night, a mad priest of Zeus broke into the quiet palace. He was desperate to take the daughter of the king of the gods and take her back to the temple. Why? Who knows? He was mad! Don't ask stupid questions!

Oh! Perhaps he wanted to marry you?! Or make you a priestess or a seer, like Pythia? Or maybe he was going to sacrifice you to the gods?! Place you on the altar, cut out your heart and innards and burnt them on a pyre. And eat your meat for his dinner!"

Thinking of this now, it strikes me as ironic that Nest would always emphasise the human sacrifice aspect of the story. Not just ironic, but sad.

Anyway, that is the story Nest told, a mixture of truth and childish imagination. It was easy to discover that there was an incident, an attempted abduction, when I was a baby, but no one would speak about it. I can hear you all shouting at me, at these words, 'perhaps it was your father come for you!" And perhaps it was, but he didn't get me, so what is the point of thinking about it.

My second abduction I remember, at least some of it. It happened around my 7th birthday. At that point, my eyes had taken on their clear green hue, and my hair was long with soft tight corkscrew curls falling around my face.

Nest would tease me that I was getting attention; we were still children, so could run free. I would laugh at this, cry how it wasn't true, how horrible it would be. But underneath that, I was… unsettled. Not quite afraid but… I did see that people were looking at me. This had happened since I could remember, but now it was followed by something more. Men would touch my arm or my hair. They would try to sit me on their laps. Nest who was never far, would always grab me before they could, and we'd run off shrieking with laughter and make it a game. I think the teasing and joking was the only way we could make it feel right.

It was a complete surprise when I was taken. I was playing with Nest and our other sisters in the shadows of the gardens, enjoying the last of the sunshine. To the best of my memory, a group of men appeared – they seemed huge and dark, but all men do to little girls, especially those coming to hurt them. I remember them knocking down Phoebe, and Nest sinking her nails into their arms, but they shook her off.

One of them had a sack and they grabbed me shoving me inside. It smelt like stale grain and grass. And later, after I wet myself, of urine.

Sometimes when I am around the stables or the granaries, something like that smell comes up and all I can do is run otherwise I freeze and cry. I don't want anyone to see that. So, I run into the house, to my room, I crawl under my bed where I know I am safe, and I breathe and scream into a scarf. It's funny because I didn't scream then. But I scream now.

I don't remember much about what happened next. I was jolted and in pain and scared. I was very scared. I know they must have taken me out of the sack. You cannot travel from Sparta to Athens without a rest stop. But I don't remember it.

I do remember when I was finally in Athens. I was scrubbed and cleaned and clothed and presented to a tall fair man in an ornate hall. A king, obviously, but I was too young to know where I was, or who I was being presented to. I was still so very scared.

Perhaps you already know. After all, it was nearly 50 years ago, and that king is another so-called hero. It was Theseus. Saviour of Athenian youth, killer of monsters, solver of riddles, seducer of princesses, abandoner of wives, and abductor of little girls.

To be fair, he seemed bemused when I was presented to him.

It turned out (as I later learnt) that fair King Theseus of Athens was on the hunt for yet another wife, having apparently lost his previous one (that made it two down if you need to keep count). He wanted a wife that would boost his credentials; he hadn't killed any monsters for a while. Rumours from Sparta were too good to pass up; a daughter of Zeus seemed just the thing, and ties to the Spartan throne made it a good opportunity even with dubious heritage. It seemed unlikely Tyndareus would agree to the marriage, so an abduction was decided on.

During all the planning, it seemed no one had considered the age of the King's new bride. Obviously, I wasn't going to be producing Zeus' grandchildren any time soon.

I've been quite harsh on Theseus. Don't get me wrong, most of his behaviour was awful. But in that moment, with me trembling in his great hall, he was kind. He dismissed his men, except for some of his advisors and the woman who would be my nurse during my stay. He ordered honey cakes and warm drinks, and he softly drew me into conversation. Welcoming me on my impromptu visit at Athens.

I was there for only a few months, though to a child it felt much longer. I had tutors to teach me to dance and to write, and even some of the daughters of prominent Athenians for company on occasion. I didn't go out much, or at all; I was kept closely guarded and few were allowed with me, but those who did were precious. Occasionally Theseus would come by. He would tell his tale to a rapt audience, and every time he told it, something would be added; the dungeons became a labyrinth, the thread turned to magic, the brutal jailor became a bull-headed monster. No one minded; if nothing else, Theseus was an excellent storyteller.

I suppose Athens is where some of those ladies and visitors first got wind of how I looked. I don't recall any comments whilst I was there, but I was so young, and it was so novel. The Athenians seemed so different anyway when compared to Sparta, sleeker, sophisticated. Different again from Troy, where power and strength oozed from the walls.

The day I left Athens, it was raining. An omen perhaps? They like omens, the Athenians. Otherwise, it was quite lowkey. Theseus had been in touch with Tyndareus, negotiating my release. I don't know the terms, and I don't want to. He already had a new wife lined up, and there was no need to wait for me.

The twins came to escort me home, along with a show of Spartan strength. It wasn't an invasion though I've heard it said it was. There was very little that happened. At least that I remember. It was a dreary journey, and immediately upon my arrival I was taken to be inspected, to ensure I was still intact.

It was the most exciting and terrifying thing to happen to me until I reached 24. I can't remember it really; I was too young. Just the coarse bag, the honey cakes, and the smiles of Theseus. But that is enough.

So, now I come to the third abduction. The one you all already know about. How does it go?

Paris is part of a delegation from Troy, comes across Helena, the most beautiful woman in the world, and falls in love. He whisks her away to Troy to marry her, an insult to his host and her true husband and the heroes of Greece rise-up to right this terrible wrong.

Or perhaps you've heard another version? Paris meets Helena, and she seduces him, as that is the way of women, especially beautiful women. She is a temptress, and she leads Paris astray, abandons her husband and children, and causes the great heroes of Greece and Troy to take up arms. It lasts ten long years because of the honeyed poison this woman drips into the ears of Paris and the Trojan men.

Or is this story? Paris declares Aphrodite the most beautiful goddess, and as a reward she gifts him the most beautiful woman in the world, Helen, casting a spell on the fair Queen. This causes the goddesses Athena and Hera take the side of the Greeks against the Trojans, and we are all nothing more than pawns in the gods petty jealousies.

There are more. A range of different stories or details. I've heard them being told by storytellers in the market, by women working and passing the time, by men deep in their cups. They are all different, but they have one common thread – that Helen left Troy with Paris. And that is the truth, though hardly all of it.

What if I told you that that delegation, that meeting, was already putting certain kings on the path to war with Troy? Would you be surprised? I don't know much about war or trade or gold, but I know they are tied together. Odysseus and Agammenon were greedy. Menelaus wanted to be seen as strong. And Paris, Priam and Hector were prideful. Did they really need more to cause a storm?

The simple answer is that I tipped it over the edge. I would agree, without me, any war might not have started so soon, or lasted so long. Or might not have been considered as glorious. What do you think would rouse the hearts of men more, a dispute over trade or the honour of a husband and all of Greece?

Paris arrived in Sparta at the end of Spring once it was safe to travel. I knew the Trojan delegation was around. I heard them more than saw them; they had no women with them, and Menelaus was wary of them. For many men having a divine beauty for a wife would be something to show off, but not to him.

I heard about the Trojans from the other women though. They liked to gossip, and some of them were enamoured with one or more of them. Some were having affairs. Though they would never talk about such things in front of me. Who knew what I would do?! But as you know, I am an excellent eavesdropper, so I heard a lot.

That was how I first heard of Paris. He was the most handsome, the most charming, the most kind. It seemed that half the palace was in love with him. I was intrigued by all our guests, so I happily asked questions about this prince and gossiped alongside them. There was even some suggestion that Paris could be a match for Hermione.

Despite all this, I was surprised to find a man in my garden one day. He was richly dressed, and very handsome. At first, I almost thought he was a boy as he had no beard, but instead a thin layer of stubble that seemed to outline his face.

It's hard to admit this, but I want to tell the truth. Or at least my truth.

I was surprised to see him, and I didn't know what to say. He told me he'd gotten turned around; he was lost. He asked me for help, he 'mistook' me for a lady, and complimented me.

In my youth I was shy. It wasn't until the end of the siege that I really found my voice. I certainly was not the powerful Queen that Nest was. I couldn't really look at him. I think I stuttered and told him I was Helena, the Queen of Sparta; I tried to seem more confident than I was. From Paris, there came a lot of words about how I couldn't possibly be – I was too young, too beautiful, too exotic, and so on.

I admit, the words turned my head a little. I'm not sure how, when I'd heard it before. I suppose, people said those things, but rarely to my face; whispers remember. Perhaps it was because we were in my place, safe in the garden; perhaps it was because Paris really did seem handsome and charming and kind; perhaps it was because Menelaus was joining someone else every night; or perhaps I am sometimes as vain as the next girl and like to hear a compliment.

Either way, I smiled at him, perhaps a little coyly, and I let him stay a while as I sketched some plants for my next tapestry.

The second time Paris showed up in the garden, it could be excused. But by the third and fourth times, it was clear he was doing this on purpose. In hindsight, I realise he must have had someone in my household in his pocket, or several someone's. He always seemed to appear when I was in the garden on my own, or only with the children.

He would often sit nearby and talk, always at a respectful distance, and eventually he began to ask me about the plants. That was clever. That was what got me to respond to him properly. I'd never really spoken to anyone about them before, except for the gardeners and kitchen staff. Anyone who did enquire clearly never really listened, even Menelaus.

But Paris asked about the different types of plants in the garden, why I was clipping some and not others, why I was clipping the parts I was, why weren't they all flowers. I answered him happily. And the way he stood, attentive, repeating parts back to me and asking more, bouncing off what I had said, well, it was nice.

That led to other conversations.

Talking of flowers led to him talking about his mother and sister. He told me stories of him and Cassandra playing in the fountains in the palace of Troy; how his sister was an annoying know-it-all he wouldn't trade for the world. Of being scolded by his mother when he and his siblings raided the kitchens and stole honey cakes. Not that it can be called stealing when the cooks give them to you. Everyone seemed to love the royal children of Troy. He told me of his elder brother and father teaching him the sword, and the debates they would have.

I told him about Nest. He mentioned he'd met her once, briefly, and he complimented her; she was also a beauty and so sharp. Complimenting Nest made me like him so much. Once she left Sparta, almost no one spoke of her. I don't even know if he really met her.

When I had Hermione or Aethiolas with me, Paris showed as much interest in them. He played with them both, and even brought a wooden sword once to battle Aethiolas. He complimented me on my maternal skills, and I thought he would make a good father. That, in a few years, he might be a good fit for Hermione.

It was…nice.

It's embarrassing to admit that I was drawn in because someone was nice to me, because it was a nice atmosphere, and a nice thing to do. But that's the truth. I think we don't want to admit how powerful that is. In a world of strength and beauty and cunning and harshness, niceness is so alluring.

I want to be clear about one thing – I never loved Paris of Troy. Never. My head was turned a little, and I enjoyed his company and talking to him. I want to emphasise that – I enjoyed talking to him. There were so few people I ever really talked to. Most people talked to me. Or at me. Even Nest would often blow past me with her eagerness. But Paris created a two-way conversation. I thought we were becoming friends.

When he pulled me into his arms and kissed me, my hesitancy came from surprise. I'd only ever been kissed by my husband and had never felt any desire to kiss anyone. I pushed him away and ran, but the damage was done.

I wish I had acted differently. If I had reported him to someone as soon as he appeared or pushed him away from me sooner, so many things would be different.

I know there are circles within circles. That war is not declared because of a kiss. That I had little control over

Paris; I never truly did. But still, how different the world might be.

Someone had been keeping an eye on us, perhaps waiting for this moment. Now I think it was one of my ladies. She was most likely Paris' informer and would be best placed to tell of our rendezvous. Did she tell due to her loyalty to Sparta or because Paris paid her? That I'll never know.

I do know that I was awoken in the dark that night. That for a moment, Paris' hand over my mouth brought back memories of the previous kidnapping, and I froze even as the desire to cry out came over me like a wave. It was like I was back in that urine-soaked sack.

That was followed by the shock of him being in my bed. A place no man other than Menelaus could be. A place he should not have been able to find, no matter how 'lost' he was.

I remember screaming, so I must have reacted, but I was outside of myself. I think that scream was more of surprise, confusion, fear, than a real call for help. Paris was cradling me in his arms and kissing my head, talking in sweet tones. I know I didn't push him away or fight. In that moment, again, frozen as I was, scared and panicked, the warmth of a body seemed safe. Even though it wasn't.

Then there was a mixture of guards and servants in my room, Trojan, and Spartan. If I'd been in my right mind, I'd have wondered why Trojan guards were so close to the women's quarters of Sparta. I do remember them, a few swarming in, then all stopping as one.

They saw us!

Paris in my bed, and me in his arms. My scream didn't matter. What they saw was enough.

Then Paris drew his sword and one of the guards went down and there was blood. So much blood. And screaming.

I remember Paris grabbing me, slapping me to calm me down.

I was shaking, and I couldn't breathe, couldn't move. I couldn't comprehend what he was saying, what was happening. Just the people and the noise, and the blood.

Paris was still speaking, but his tone was changing. From soft and gentle, to stone hard as marble. This is what happens when Paris wants something and doesn't get what he wants.

"If you stay here, they'll kill you" His words dropped like a pit into my stomach, piercing through my panic.

I didn't want to die. But even I knew what this would look like.

I didn't think of Menelaus or how I might talk to him – I didn't think of talking to anyone.

I did try to go to my children; I hope you believe that. My first clear thought was that I would have to take them with me, but Paris wouldn't let me. They weren't mine after all, they belonged to Menelaus, and we would have more. His tone went back to a caress once he knew I was doing what he wanted. He hugged me and kissed me and told me everything would be fine. I would be his wife now and he would protect me from Menelaus and Agamemnon and anyone else.

Sparta is landlocked; the sea is not close, but Troy is far away, going all the way overland was too dangerous, even without a princess in a sack. Going by ship is the only way the royal house of Troy travels. Paris bundled me into a cart and held me as it headed towards the sea. I was frozen in his arms, I felt the panic and fear, but couldn't do anything about it. I was a 7-year-old girl again, being dragged across Greece in a sack.

Then we reached the sea. It was the smell that hit me first; I'd never been on the sea, never really been near it. There was a ship, which seemed huge to me, but I now know was moderately sized. He carried me into the bowels of the ship, and we set sail in no time.

I realise now that you can't just set sail; that there need to be winds and currents and tides. That a cart won't be idling in the middle of the night near a palace for no reason. How much time did he spend planning it? When did he decide? I suppose it doesn't matter.

He left me in a small cabin, on a hard wooden bed, where I know I sat cold and rigid. Everything had happened so quickly. My brain was starting to catch up.

It was sometime later that Paris returned to the cabin. He pulled me into his lap, stroking my hair, wiping my tears. Shushing me. He kept telling me how much he loved me, how beautiful I was, and how when we got to Troy, we would be man and wife. How happy I would make him.

Nothing about how happy he would make me.

All I could think about was my daughter, my son, my loom, my garden. What would happen to them?

III. Troy

Sparta doesn't have walls. It has never had walls and it will never have walls. Sparta does not need walls because its men make it invulnerable. I'm sure one day that will be put to the test, and one day it will fail.

I say this so that you can understand how completely awed I was when we approached Troy.

When I think of Troy, I can still feel that awe and that sense of wonder.

You could see the city from far away; a white speck that got bigger as we approached. Surrounded by a deep dark blue that turned lighter and greener as the speck got bigger. Paris could barely endure standing on the ship; the sea did not agree with him, and he spent most of his time below decks. I got to see Troy first on my own.

I found the sea more than agreed with me. I enjoyed the sharp spray on my face, the brine smell, and the clear skies. Perhaps my father was really Poseidon?! The idea he was Zeus, just misdirection. I still love the water, any type of water. I love the river, but I do sometimes miss the tangy salt of the sea.

That journey was an in-between time. A time when you are neither in one place nor another, you are not your old self of before but haven't yet become the person of the future. We weren't in Sparta; we weren't at Troy. We were suspended in time and space, and it felt good. I remember feeling good; there were no problems, no consequences. The sea kept everything at bay.

Some of the biggest moments of life happened during those in-between times. Its where decisions are made, actions begin. For me, those in-between times are some of the most important and memorable of my life.

Like watching that dot on the horizon grow bigger and bigger and bigger. As we drew closer, I realised I was looking at the ring of a huge stone wall. It was grey and beaten with plants growing from cracks, and the sea was lashing against it, like it was trying to get in. I felt the weight of those walls fall on my shoulders. I felt the power of them encircle me.

You're probably hoping that I'll tell you all about the vibrant docks, the range of people, even give a detailed plan of the city. I can't.

It was a very long time ago and I never really saw it. But I do remember the immensity; everything about Troy was huge. Now I know there are bigger, grander, more impressive structures in the world, but none of them compared to Troy in my mind. I remember a general sense of a rush, people everywhere, the loud sounds and screeches, the smell of food, spices, and horseshit. It was overwhelming; after so many days at sea, it was almost too much.

Besides, even Paris knew it was inadvisable to linger on the docks with the queen you've kidnapped. It is much more sensible to get her inside and away from prying eyes.

I was bundled onto another cart, and was pulled through the city, my only real glimpse through the swaying gaps in the curtain that covered us. The place was paved, the streets were organised, the buildings were tall. I could feel the wealth of Troy in the bones of the city; everywhere was rich and beautiful and big. Of course, I wouldn't have been taken through the darker, danker, dangerous parts of the city; I know now that every city has somewhere like that. But I can't help but think that even those parts were probably splendid compared to elsewhere.

I admit it, I did like Troy. Or those pieces I saw. It was so different from Sparta, so new and exotic. And in my mind, it stays like that, there's no way to change it.

Then I saw we were being ushered through gates and gates and gates and through a wall that seemed as thick as any I'd known. Finally, I knew I was in a palace. There was a hush in there completely different from anywhere else. There were slaves and servants, a controlled bustle that I was familiar with, and things were…lush. More so than Sparta. Everything seemed richer, cooler, hotter, darker, lighter. Lush.

I wish I could tell you more. Give a map of the city, tell you how it felt and looked, what the people were like, where the temples stood. But the only time I really saw Troy, it was on fire.

The House of Priam

It was that first day, that first hour in Troy, that I met the royal family, the house of Priam.

They were waiting for us. It's amazing how quickly news can travel, though Paris couldn't be sure what the news would say or who it would come from. I never found out exactly what they had heard, but they were ready for us. Ready for me.

I was brought into a large circular room, and there they stood, arranged before me. A perfect tableau of wealth, beauty, and power.

I recognised Hector from my father's funeral; he was older, fuller, stronger. He looked a lot like Paris, but where Paris was pretty, Hector was handsome, where Paris was lean and delicate, Hector was all thick muscle and hard edge. He treated me that day much as he would every day; his gaze slid over me, away from me. Away from temptation? Away from the cause of all his ills? I don't know. I'm not even sure he ever spoke to me; I cannot recall a single conversation or uttered word whilst I lived in the palace. It was only when I was a foreign queen, not his sister-in-law that he ever engaged with me.

Did he die for me? This man who never came near, who kept his distance. No, he died for Troy. They called him the Son of Troy, their golden prince. Paris might have been his mother's favourite, but Hector was the man the people loved. Maybe more than Priam. And he returned that love. Thinking on it, perhaps it's good that he died before the end of the war. He didn't have to see the city fall.

The presence of the women in the room surprised me. That would never happen at Sparta. Troy felt looser, easier with its women than Sparta. We still had our quarters, but the others did venture outside the palace walls, and conferred with their men. That wasn't for me though; I wouldn't leave that palace until I was fleeing Troy itself.

I think Andromache gave Hector much council when no one was around; it seemed he would always go to bed with questions and wake up with answers. She was standing right next to him in that hall, a little behind, her hand protectively placed over her slightly swollen stomach. I think she knew then that that baby would never be king of Troy. I never saw what happened to him, but I heard the stories. I'd say I can't imagine her pain, but I know it perfectly well.

She was lovely to look at, Andromache, and it was a love match, her and Hector. It radiated off them, even at that moment as they stood firm and powerful. You could see it in the way they glanced at each other, in the soft caress of an arm, a brief touch of the fingers. It never stopped. I envied them, that intimacy, that familiarity. When their son Astyanax was sick, Hector stayed with Andromache throughout the night. When my children died, Paris disappeared. I suppose we all grieve in our own ways.

I would sit at the loom with Andromache next to me. I don't think she was spying on me, there were plenty of others to do that, but every time I saw her, she'd ask me how I was feeling. She never asked me anything else, never sought me out or invited me to her rooms. She never asked how I was, not how had my day been or how the children were. She only ever asked, how was I feeling?

Of course, I lied. I couldn't let her know how I really felt. And of course, she knew that. Except when my children died. She didn't ask me then. But Andromache stayed with me as no one else could, as a fellow mother, wife, pawn in the world of men. But not as a friend, I don't think. Almost anything but that. As I wailed and sobbed and turned silent, she fed me, bathed me, and held me. She supported me as we buried them, literally holding me up. I can barely remember it; I was so lost. But I remember her being there. Eventually, she resumed asking that same question, but only once my answer was no longer a wail; it was still there, all that grief and guilt, but trapped in some deep, dark place inside. I found it was easy to lie again.

It was our ritual.

At least until Hector died. Then she disappeared. I wanted to go to her, to support her as she did me, but I couldn't. I didn't have that strength, that feeling, and besides, with Hector gone, Paris was now the heir presumptive, and I had more to think about than a kindly ghost's dead husband. That Andromache shunned everyone around her made it easier to ignore her. She spent all her time in his tomb pulling her hair and wailing, many of us swore we could hear it echoing through the walls of the palace, perhaps they even heard it in the Greek camp? They might as well have bricked her up in it with him.

She wasn't the only woman in the room when I arrived. Jocasta was there too, hand on Priam's shoulder, possessive, as though since I'd taken one man, I might take hers too. She looked so much like Paris, and he ran to her the moment we entered the room, her expression softening for an instant. Paris was her favourite and could do no wrong in her eyes. Me, she viewed with suspicion, never truly trusting me.

Before my wedding to Paris, only a week after we arrived, she was the one who calmed me down. I must have looked pale, as pale as I can look, and I know my eyes were wet. She sent everyone away, even Andromache who gave us a curious glance as she left us alone.

I remember her words to me clearly. "These are not time for tears or for feeling sorry for yourself. This is a mess of your own making. You are Trojan now. You are to be Paris' wife. You must keep him happy and healthy. You will be one of us." The way she said it, I wonder now if she was saying it as much to herself as to me.

I nodded, and I felt the tears spill. It was odd because I did not really feel sorry for myself. I didn't think that was what I was feeling. It was more like a memory, a jolt, that was causing my tears; the same as on the cart the night Paris took me. The wedding clothes, the palace, the women fluttering around me, even the idea of my groom waiting for me; they made me think of that sack from childhood. Like I was again being snatched away, held prisoner, terrified and alone. It made no sense.

"Don't cry" it was a command, not a suggestion, "you'll make your eyes red and ruin your face; it'll make your cheeks look even more round."

Jocasta must have seen something in my face following that, as she softened slightly. "This is the way of the world. You obviously like him, after some fashion. There must be something there or this would not have happened. Use that something for yourself, and for Paris. That will make him happy. Be what he needs. And what Paris needs, is someone to adore him. Do that, use that, and it will make you happy. It will make Troy happy."

"Is that what you do?" the words slipped out before I could stop myself. I remember the look she gave me. Her eyes narrowed and her lips pursed, but then turned into a cruel smile.

"Isn't that what we all do?" she asked back. "Besides, Priam has never been Paris. And I am not you. Now smile."

So, I did. Through my tears, I smiled as sweetly, as meaningfully, as I could. But Jocasta had a similar view as Tyndareus though. She wrinkled her nose as she looked at me and said, "Actually don't. You look better with no teeth showing."

She swished away.

The Trojan women always seemed so adept at swishing.

Paris' younger two siblings were there as well, at my greeting or judgement. Deiphobus, was lurking next to his mother. Or perhaps that's just how I see him in my mind. He was only about 20 on that first meeting, but that corner of my memory is darker. He resembled his brothers, but instead of the charm and delicacy of Paris, he had malice and sycophancy; the heroism and bravery of Hector he twisted into cunning and spite. But maybe my mind is poisoning the memory with hindsight. The thought of his fingers on my skin, the sour hiss in my ear still makes me shudder though he is long dead.

I was almost married to him after Paris died; I had no choice about it. As a widow with no children, Troy had to keep me close – I was the reason for the war after all. And just like in some play, the younger brother, the lesser brother, tried to make up for everything he thought he wasn't. It never happened. Deiphobus didn't fit into Hector's armour, nor did he lie easy in Paris' bed. I think that was always his fate.

It's odd that out of this family of heroes, I think the youngest girl might now be the most famous. It's funny what parts of the story, which characters, the storytellers latch on to, who they select to tell tales about on a market square. Her name seems to fall off people's tongues like a common saying; everyone knows you must be wary of Cassandra's prophecies, all doom and gloom and, worst of all, true. They weren't prophecies though; she could not see the future. I've heard that Odysseus is often given the moniker swift or some such. He was clever and cunning, but he strikes me mostly as lucky. Cassandra is the one who had a truly swift mind. She seemed to be able to see problems and solve them before anyone else before they even occurred. I think she might have been the cleverest person in the world and was called mad because of it.

On that day though, she was still young, acting even younger. She must have been around 15, yet she sat at her father's feet like a little girl, she even had a doll in her lap. At her age I was married, trying to get pregnant, shaming my husband's mistress. She was the only one who looked at me with open fascination. Like she wanted to drink up every part of me.

Though I first met her as a girl, my main memory of her is as a woman; angry and defiant and screaming at her father, her brother, anyone around her that it was foolish to bring in that wooden horse.

"The Greeks were at our gates, they've taken our defender, why would they leave?" She shrieked, her anger radiating off her in red waves. That did not help her cause.

I recall her father trying to calm her, he told her that the Greeks had taken their pound of flesh and now all was well.

"You think Hector for a whore a fair trade?" She yelled. Priam slapped her.

It was the only time I ever saw him lose his temper and it was the briefest of flashes. A sudden bolt that for a moment showed the powerful man he used to be. It shocked Cassandra to silence, and she was ushered away. Perhaps I should have been stung by that comment, we became sort of friends, or at least friendly, but her world was falling apart. Besides, maybe she was right about me. I played my role after all.

As we all know, she was right about that horse.

Cassandra was always right.

Cassandra would listen at doors, hide in corridors, gossip with servants and slaves. She told me once it was gathering information, so she could understand what was going on. And it worked. She always did seem to know what was going on, what strategy was in use next, what disaster the next battle would bring. I suppose she was a lot like Nest in that way. And like myself, though I was never so bold to brag about what I had learned, I would keep any secrets to myself. Perhaps that's why I liked her so much, despite everything. She is what I could have been or wanted myself to be if I'd had the courage.

She would often be seen at her father's and brother's side, whispering into their ears, trying to make them listen.

No one ever listened to her though.

And finally, sitting on a throne, flanked by his family, with his advisors and servants, sat Priam. You could see how he would have mirrored Hector in his prime; his muscles were still there but were less pronounced, and his hair and beard were grey. By the end of the war, they would be white, and he would be thin, bent, decimated. But then, in that room, he was at his height; he was king, he was surrounded by a beautiful and devoted family, and it was him that was going to seal my fate.

Priam Deciding

The events that took place in that room still echo in my mind. I can feel the heat from the braziers with the eddies of cool air that drifted around my arms from behind me. I can feel the stares of everyone in that room, assessing, judging, the smell of bodies and flame, the headiness of the scenario. If I close my eyes, I can see it all play out again.

"What have you done?" It was Hector; it would always be Hector. Paris started babbling, and Hector started shouting, Andromache trying to quiet them, Jocasta shaking Priam to do something, Deiphobus smirking and sniping. Then the advisors started chipping in. Soon almost all of them were wrapped up in the argument about my presence. Did Paris know what he'd done? Were they ready for war? What kind of ransom would be required? Already there were envoys en route from Sparta, from Mycenae – what would be done?

I was quite used to being talked about and talked around, so I let them get on with it. Though I realised that there were two people not shouting, not saying anything. Cassandra, sitting at her father's feet, continued to just look at me, to take me in, like she was processing all the different things this could mean. But she was just a girl, and no one would have listened to her anyway.

Her gaze though, was mirrored by Priam, who simply sat on his throne, surrounded by his red-faced family, and looked at me.

I decided to look back.

I don't know why. Up to that point, and the years after, I would avert my gaze. Keep my eyes downcast, dutiful, meek, serene. But this time, in that room, with the king of Troy looking at me, I decided to meet his eyes. Perhaps I understood that I needed to do that, that my life rested with that man, and the only thing I could do was meet him head on.

He smiled and though his family's voices were bouncing off the walls, his calm, low voice managed to cut through them all. "Please leave us. I wish to talk to the Queen of Sparta alone".

Both Hector and Paris tried to object, but what were they going to do? Priam just smiled indulgently at them and repeated his request. Everyone filed out, and I mean everyone, leaving just me and the King of Troy alone.

I remember my breath caught in my throat. I had no idea what was going to happen, or what I should say. Should I plead my case to be sent home? Should I beg to stay? What would you have done?

And then Priam took me by complete surprise. "Would you care for some wine?"

I nodded a yes, and he surprised me further by climbing off his throne, walking towards a small table, and pouring me a cup himself. As he handed it to me, I saw his smile didn't reach his eyes. "Now, what are we going to do?"

I gulped the wine and shook my head. I remember it was oddly sweet and thick, a shock to my senses. I recall whispering 'I don't know' as tears stung my eyes.

Priam sighed. There was so much in that sigh. Perhaps I'm placing more emphasis on it than there was; seeing things in the past that weren't there. But it feels now like in that sigh, he knew what would happen.

"Helena. Is that your name? Did my son bring you here of your own free will?"

I considered for a moment. That question, one that haunts me. Did I choose to come, agree to it? No. Did I stop it?

No. Had I accepted it? Yes. Did it really matter now I was here? No.

"Yes." I said weakly.

Priam raised he eyebrows at me.

He wanted more. He needed more. He needed to understand what had happened, and from my perspective, so he could decide what to do. I took a deep breath, choosing my words carefully.

"I did scream, but I also came with him when he asked. I didn't scream after that." I knew what was important, what mattered. All that mattered was that I came, even if I'd been in shock, in some kind of trance, I was found with him in my bed. I hadn't tried to stop him.

Priam was listening intently. It seemed like he expected more, but already knew everything that had happened. He sighed again.

"And what now, Helena?"

"I suppose that is up to you."

Priam nodded and started pacing. He started talking but I'm not sure it was really to me. "You understand this is a precarious situation, yes? It will be unlikely that Menelaus will be happy if I just send you back. He'll want reparation. And he'll want it in blood as well as gold. And even if he forgoes the blood, he could bankrupt us."

Whilst he paced, I thought of what would happen to me if I were sent back. Would I die? Would I remain queen? Would I stay at the palace? Would I see my children? Did I want that? Even now it's hard to know what I would have chosen. My children, yes, but my husband and the throne?

It was all I knew, and it wasn't a bad life, but even then, I'm not sure I would want to go back. Though the alternative was obviously to stay with Paris.

Perhaps if I'd never seen the sea, the idea of another life would never have occurred to me.

For Priam there was no consideration of that. Of what this decision would mean to me. It didn't matter.

Priam was still talking. "And not to mention what Paris has done. We'll not be trusted again. But if I don't send you back…now what would that mean? I could buy them off. Or more likely they'll bring their soldiers. I feel another's hand behind this. I should have sent Hector. We were so close to peace. Now…I see war at my gate. And it comes with such a pretty face."

He stopped in front of me and looked at me. "Such a pretty face" he repeated, reaching out like he would touch me. He stopped himself at the last moment. It took all my strength not to flinch.

"And what do you want?"

I was taken aback. I didn't know. I told him so. He considered this, rephrased the question. "What do you think would be best for you?"

That was more straightforward. There was no obvious answer, it was all unknowns, and I had no time to think, and no experience of making such decisions. I'd escaped death due to indiscretion once, I'm not sure my luck would hold out a second time. All I could do was follow the path already laid out before me. So, I told Priam that for me, staying with Paris, behind these walls would be the safest thing. Or so I thought.

"But that is a very expensive choice." Priam hissed. "It will bring soldiers to my door. How am I to keep everyone safe? Shouldn't I toss you out the gate? Let Menelaus do with you what he sees fit?"

Fear reared up inside me; the base fear of death and dishonour and not knowing the future. It was everything that had slipped past me while I was out at sea. I thought of Menelaus' hands on my throat, the ease with which he took lovers and fathered children, his rash brother who left my sister patterned in purple. Priam may have already decided what he wanted to do by that point, had already put plans in motion, but it felt in that moment, that I had to fight for myself. I'd never done that before.

"No! No, you should not. If I am to be blamed, then so is Paris. You said so yourself. If tossing me away delays war, it does not stop it." I wasn't sure if I was saying the right things.

Priam gave me a small smile. "You're not wrong. This has been brewing for longer than you've been alive. But still, time is a precious gift in such cases. And I still need to ready my men."

"I can pay for that. I can pay for myself."

That got his attention. I could feel his gaze on me again, but this time it was different. He was trying to figure out how I could pay for myself. I couldn't help but smile myself, feeling the fear fade slightly, knowing I had a trick up my sleeve, or in my seams. Something that had been drilled into me since I was 7 years old was finally paying off.

After my abduction to Athens, a woman of the court had given me some advice. She had similar skin and hair to me and spoke with an unusual accent. I was young and hadn't noticed her before. But she told me the world was dangerous for girls like us, and what had happened once could happen again, especially if I was taken beyond Greece, far from the cities who might have heard of me; anything could happen. To ensure my own survival, she advised sewing jewels or other precious items into my clothes. All my clothes. She told me to wear bracelets along my arms, chains at my neck, and to pin my hair. My gold and jewellery were so delicate, it was easy advice to follow; I sewed a fortune into my wardrobe.

"There is one language that is universal, and everything has a price, even freedom" her smile had been sad then. I saw her only a few more times, then she left with her husband, a trader, to explore other lands.

But I listened.

I bedecked myself with jewels and gold, and everything I could think of. I wore them whilst at the loom, in the garden, even at night as I slept. Those I did not wear, I sewed into my dresses, created small purses, and found space across my body to secure and secrete precious things. I was after all, an excellent seamstress, and there's only so many shirts and dresses and shrouds one can make before you turn to other things.

I wore those items with half an eye to the future, to my safety, but it was something my father and husband loved. All my husbands loved seeing me like that. They were delighted that I decked myself out, showed off their wealth and strength. The other women were not so keen, though they added to my collection; I was often gifted jewellery or other trinkets, growing my collection. As I look back now, I think this trick of mine added to all those stories of

Helena the Vain, Helena the Manipulator, Helena the Whore.

So, when Priam was looking for a reason to keep me, I knew I could pay him for my life. First, I pulled the jewellery from my arms, my neck, my legs, even my toes; bracelets, necklaces, rings. Next, I grabbed at my nightdress, pulling at the hidden pockets. Last, I delicately unclasped the brooch that sat casually on the end of my stole. It was the swan brooch I'd found in my mother's jewellery box. I always wore it. Always.

I had to hold this horde in the drape of my dress, there was so much, and it was heavy. Removing it all, I felt lighter. I hadn't even realised how much it had weighed me down.

Priam stared at my hands in awe.

"Will this do?" I whispered.

At that moment, Paris barged back into the room. He was ready to run away and abandon Troy rather than leave me. Priam cut him off.

"Calm yourself boy. Your wife will stay. We at Troy do not throw women out on their heels. And we do not stand in the way of true love" Priam winked at me as he carefully picked up one of the jewels from my hands. I barely noticed the room slowly filling, a servant coming forward to take the load from me.

As he leaned in to kiss my cheek he muttered "You are ours now. You are Trojan. You will give us everything." He pushed something cold into my hands as he did so.

I'm not sure if anyone else noticed. Paris was crying hurrah and he swept me into his arms while the rest of the family looked on. Once settled I looked at what Priam has given me.

It was the swan brooch. I was Trojan, I had become Trojan, but I was still Helena. I was still something more. Perhaps my arguments, my jewels had not swayed Priam at all. Perhaps it had been something else entirely?

Could I have gone home? Maybe. But I was afraid. And I wanted to be safe. In that way I did choose Troy over Sparta, infamy over family. I'd heard enough to know that war was on the horizon whether I stayed or not. I decided to bet on Troy. As you know that was the wrong horse.

War

Is there any life that has not been touched by war?

From the moment we're born, we're destined to either fight in one or mourn in one, or both. Even die in one. War is what made my birth so special, and it's what has made me, made everyone, famous.

How do I talk about that? How do I break down the war? Explain my life for the next 8 or 9 years?

I suppose I should tell you what happened next. The dance that had to take place so everyone could say they were in the right, despite everyone knowing the outcome of all this.

There had to be envoys and talks, attempts at reconciliation, offers of peace, each side trying to pretend to appease the other, or throwing accusations.

I didn't see any of it.

But I felt it. The way the air seemed to become heavier. The entire city froze with tension, and everyone seemed to be holding their breath.

It strikes me as I write this, that most of my life hasn't been about seeing. Just as the sound snipping at my heels has always been whispers, my own experiences have been made up of other senses; hearing, smelling, feeling. I have seen very little of what happened around me, because of me, but I've sensed it, felt it. When I close my eyes to remember something, I find it hard to conjure up the images. I have a vague memory of the richness of Troy, but I don't have a clear view. Not when I try, when I focus on that moment. But a memory can come anytime through other means; a whiff of spice, the feel of a dress, the sound of metal scraping metal, and I can clearly recall the feeling and actions of a certain moment.

Is it like that for everyone? Or is it just me? Or just age playing one of its many tricks?

I was still adjusting to the palace at Troy then. It was big and lush and rich and almost silent to me. Silent because people seemed scarce around me; few crossed my path, and I was turned away from rooms and spaces – people always seemed to be just round the corner. Almost silent, because the one sound that echoed everywhere was that of the soldiers: of men and boys practising in every courtyard and open space throughout the city. In fact, the palace seemed almost devoid of men; there were never that many whilst I lived there.

Those sounds were the only real sense I got of what was happening.

I had never been particularly loud, but I found myself sighing, singing, and even screaming in my room just to feel heard. Even if only by myself and the stern maid who followed me everywhere. Jailer? Bodyguard? Harem mistress? It doesn't much matter. I ignored her as much as I could.

I still didn't see much of anyone at first, I mostly sat in my rooms, usually at the loom. My rooms were bigger than at Sparta, with more of them, but hidden away. The windows overlooked internal courtyards, I was kept away from the wider world, hidden in the bowels of the palace, as labyrinthine as Sparta, but bigger, brighter, bolder. Even after Paris and I were married, only a few days after we arrived, it took time for me to be properly introduced to the Trojan court.

If I hadn't been able to sense the change in atmosphere in the palace, I didn't have to wait long to be told. Cassandra could always be relied upon to deliver whatever news she knew, though at that point, I didn't know how good she was at collecting it.

I'd only been in Troy a few weeks, and she came, dancing gracefully, into my rooms with flowers in her hair. I remember thinking how child-like she was, how she should be married, but maybe that was the problem. She already had an amazing sense of self. Power in knowing she was the baby, the favourite.

She settled herself on a cushion on the floor. It should have made her seem powerless, sitting beneath me, like the ladies at Sparta, but with her, with her uncanny gaze, it changed the centre of the room. I felt like I was revolving around her.

"So, you've noticed what's going on?" She began, "they're all there. Talking. Sometimes they even talk about you."

"Who is they?" I asked.

"The kings of Greece of course. They've come. Hector says we've never seen so many great men together in one place. Father says very few of those men are great, but they are here in person, so he knows it means war."

"We already knew that" I mumbled, distracted as I thought this through.

I was surprised they came in person and didn't send envoys. I wanted to know who was here, who made up 'the kings of Greece'. "Your father and brother talk to you about these things?"

Cassandra smiled and sighed. "They talk, and I listen. I'm very good at listening. I'm very good at being in the right place to listen. And then I think about what I've heard. I'm also very good at thinking."

I swallowed. "So, Menelaus is here."

I don't know what I wanted her answer to be. The thought of seeing him again make me queasy, and I thought again of that night he'd wrapped his hands around my throat. Nowadays, he was seen as a peaceful man, a retired soldier, and for most of our marriage he had been that, but that power and rage and skill was still there.

Cassandra nodded. "He's such an old man! I can't believe you married him. You look much finer with Paris. And he doesn't say much. He doesn't talk at all. Two others do all the talking."

“Agamemnon and Odysseus” the answer was obvious. I felt a short stab as I thought of Nest.

Cassandra nodded and grinned, apparently delighted I could figure that out myself. “Paris thinks they’re here to try to get you away, that’s why they’ve come in person. But I don’t think that’s true. Neither do father or Hector. We think that’s just a ruse. They want to go to war with Troy, they want to defeat us. They don’t really care about you. Whether we give you up, keep you, or kill you, they’ll get their wish.”

I could feel her watching me as I took this in, let it churn in my mind.

“I think they’ll be surprised though.” Cassandra continued, twirling her hair round her fingers. “They say Troy’s walls have stood for a hundred years. They’ll never breach them, so they’ll never win. It would take an act from the gods to do that.”

“Or something very cunning” I muttered, again not paying full attention to her, lost in my own thoughts. She must have heard me though, as her response made me start.

Cassandra smiled at me, showing all her teeth. “Yes, something very cunning.”

Perhaps Cassandra wasn’t that different when she was a child. Perhaps I just didn’t see her clearly.

Just as I could tell from the air around me that something was happening at Troy, I felt it when it was over. It relaxed, became clearer. The immediate danger passed. Most importantly, I was suddenly allowed out. Well, out of my rooms. From then on, I joined the women of the palace at their looms, with musicians and wine. Andromache was often there at first, getting rounder and rounder, but Jocasta rarely visited. As the war progressed, the number of women diminished as fewer men came home.

As I think back, I realise, no one actually told me that Troy had gone to war. It was just a fact, that seeped through walls, through the city. It was known.

It was a few weeks later that I was startled awake by a scream. And I swear this is true; the only time I have truly wondered if the gods exist or if that invisible link between sisters can be made solid. In the hazy dawn of that day, I jolted awake at what sounded like a scream of pain. Absolute, endless, soul-destroying pain. A scream that almost split me in two and left me breathless and shaking in my bed. A bad dream, Paris murmured into my ear as he pulled me down, and lazily started caressing me, but the feelings of pain and dread refused to subside; they dragged me down, causing me to start at small things, lose track of what I was doing.

It was over the next few days the rumours started to trickle in.

Agamemnon was determined to defeat Troy, to arrive as soon as possible. To secure favourable winds, he'd made a sacrifice. A terrible sacrifice that broke his wife's heart and mind.

Agamemnon had sacrificed his own daughter.

It was dismissed by many. To do such a thing was an abomination, an affront to the gods that would not go unpunished. It was discussed with glee by others, a good story to share over a drink, a sign of just how scared Agamemnon must be of Troy.

It was Cassandra who told me this rumour. She would stop by the women's rooms every day and tell us some of what she heard. The other women encouraged her, whilst I wondered why she wasn't staying to join us. I could tell she was only sharing titbits, that she was showing off; it quickly dissipated. But that day I could feel her watching me closely as she told us. As the women around me started muttering and fluttering. I'm sure she noticed the way my muscles froze as I remembered the awful scream and my mind flew to Nest.

"I think it's true" Cassandra often sat next to me if she had a juicy piece of gossip – wanting my reaction I suppose. Her tone told me she wasn't lying, she wasn't saying this just to provoke or tease. "I think he's just the type to do it. He'll regret it. No matter what happens here, that is something that does not go unpunished. I've heard your sister has a bit of a temper."

I thought back to those years when we were young, and Nest swore she'd kill a husband who strayed from her. We'd laughed it off, and Agamemnon was alive, so she hadn't followed through. But what might she do if he had murdered their daughter.

"And she looks very good in red," I said under my breath.

Cassandra gave me that cunning grin again and giggled.

I swear this really happened, that conversation between the mad and bad princesses of Troy.

You probably know what happened to Nest; her story sits alongside my own, one to scare men about how dangerous women can be. Though her's is nowhere near as popular. They say that she waited those long years while Agamemnon was in Troy, and when he returned, she killed him. Stabbing and drowning him with her lover. Agamemnon's punishment for killing his daughter, and then poor Nest was killed by her own son. Round and round the punishments go.

I have heard it said that Cassandra was taken by Agamemnon, that she was in that palace in Mycenae as Nest took her revenge. I wonder if Nest was the only woman to watch Agamemnon die? I think Cassandara would also have looked good in red.

Still, that was all yet to come. At that moment in Troy, there was that scream and those rumours. That scream that jolted me aware. Even, now, when I wake in the night, sweating and gasping and afraid, that is the sound I hear echoing in my head. Despite everything else I've gone through, it's not the sound of horses or boats or sizzling fire that sends me a cold sweat. It's that scream.

Once they had all gone, once the charade of diplomacy had passed, it happened quite quickly. By the end of the month, the ships started arriving. They were a spot in the distance, more a disruption of the blue sea than a real image themselves. An inversion of how Troy had looked to me. The Trojan fleet also disappeared. Smoke appeared on the horizon. The main port, attached to the city, was barricaded. Hector left and returned with dark circles under his eyes and cuts on his arms. People started streaming into the city.

Then one day, it wasn't just a line of ships, but a field of tents. And then, the sparkle of shields in the sun. And then the rumour that the famed Achilles had joined the Greeks.

And that was when the war really began.

Do you want to know a terrible thing about war? Or at least, the terrible thing about my war? The thing that causes me to feel sick as I think about it. It's the monotony. Even terror can become monotonous. You cannot stay terrified constantly, so you fall into something else.

My days in Troy at war were not that much different from those at Sparta in peace if I am honest.

I woke, I ate, I sat at my loom, I worked at a garden. At night Paris would come to me.

I became pregnant very quickly – a sign of favour from the gods – and that progressed without any complications. And two years later it happened again.

There were festivals and birthdays and seasons. Even as the army camp on the shoreline grew, these things continued as life always does.

I was not privy to the discussions of war, though again Cassandra would delight in telling me what she heard, or what she wanted me to know. Even as she grew into herself, became womanlier, she still managed to glean information, still managed to avoid the usual womanly duties. Perhaps we all let her because she gave us that information. Because keeping things as they were before felt important.

She was a great fan of games.

The women of Troy, though perhaps having more autonomy than I had in Sparta, still spent most of their time in their quarters, sewing clothes or working the loom. Cassandra was terrible with any of our womanly activities;

her mother would joke that any husband or children of Cassandra would be starving and naked.

But a board game, that was something that Cassandra loved. Though it was hard for her to find people to play with. Priam and Paris would give her a moment, but few others. They knew Cassandra would win. And Cassandra would crow about winning.

She didn't often seek me as a partner, only when she was desperate, but when she did, I always agreed. We would often play Petteia, though it was considered a man's game. For Cassandra I think that was the challenge. For me, it mattered little if anyone thought I was too masculine; it would be used as a point of pride or as a slur no matter what I did.

I recall playing her numerous times in Troy, but one time sticks out the most. She was older then, 20 or so, though less war weary than the rest of us; she always seemed to relish the war.

"You're quite good."

She was trying to decide on her next move.

"So are you" I told her.

"I'm better than quite. And so are you" she said the last bit with a sigh, like it was painful to admit. "You're cleverer than you look".

I was stumped by this. No one had ever said I was clever. It had never even been inferred. Even Nest had never said anything about my mind. Everyone commented on my beauty; that was what made me special.

"Don't look so gormless. You clearly have a strong mind. You're smart. You can think, but you choose not to. You stay quiet and you simper and pout and hide. You're so difficult to read. You never turn thinking into acting. I find it infuriating."

I didn't know what to say. I suppose that instinct she was talking about was kicking in. The instinct to stay quiet and see what happens. To survive.

I did notice she'd echoed something Nest had once said. "Perhaps that is the best way to survive. To hide, to be quiet. Perhaps I wouldn't be here if I hadn't done those things?"

Cassandra paused for a moment but continued. "Maybe. Though I know that the reason you're here is because of what you said to father that day" I knew what day she meant. Perhaps she was right? "But that seems to have been a one-off. You can do it, you just...don't. The whole world thinks you're sitting in Troy, wrapping the royal men around your little finger. And what's hilarious is that it's the opposite! You're doing nothing and they're digging their own holes. But I think you can. So, why don't you? Why don't you use your power to control them?"

I thought back over my time with Menelaus, my time with Paris, the conversations of Odysseus, the looks of Tyndareus, that moment with Priam, the whispers at my back and comments to my face.

"Because it's a false power," I said finally. "It's not real, and it's easily lost".

Cassandra considered this, then shook her head. She had another answer, a better one. "I think it's because you see yourself as flawed. As something that is in danger, that if you make the wrong move, you'll be punished, or killed. And you know what, you might be right. But that's the same for all of us. And for the sake of the gods, I hope you change that one day."

She gulped down the last of her wine at that moment. Some of this might have been spurred by drink, but most of it was just Cassandra. Brash, impulsive, and always right. Those comments were so close to what I had thought as I'd stood before Priam on my first day at Troy, it was almost comical. I spent a long time pondering those words, thinking what it meant, what I would need to do differently if I didn't want this to always be my truth.

There was one aspect of my day that I both longed for and dreaded. A command from Priam, for which I was only excused when I was in the birthing chamber. And even then, I wonder if he'd been able to enter and pull me out, whether he would have.

At the command of the king of Troy, every day I walked the walls of the city. The first part delighted me; I would stand on the walls and look out over the sea, feeling the wind in my face and smelling the brine. It was lovely. But the feeling would fade as I made my circuit. Because Priam did not command it so I could enjoy myself. Every day I stopped where the generals and king gathered, looking at the distant shore, at the line of soldiers camped so close.

A quiet would fall on everyone as I approached. They would politely nod my way. I would stand with Priam and look out across the battlements. Sometimes Hector or Deiphobus were there. Hector would ignore me, and Deiphobus would lurk. If Paris was there, he would smile and sigh and pull me to him talking on about what was happening.

That is where I was standing when I saw the two sides advance, where I heard the clashing of shields and smelt the scent of blood.

That is where I was standing when the rain poured so hard the plain turned into a muddy river and you could hear men drowning in it.

That is where I was standing when the putrid smell of decay drifted over on the wind.

That is where I was standing when the sun baked the earth, dried the wells and all that could be seen was dust.

That is where I was standing when I watched Paris fall, and, as the wind picked up, he turned tail and ran.

That is where I was standing when Hector dealt the fatal blow, only to discover the man under the helmet was not who he thought it was.

That is where I was standing when Hector was killed by Achilles.

I watched with Priam and Jocasta as their son was mercilessly stabbed over and over, stripped, lashed to the back of a chariot, and dragged. Some say Achilles rode the chariot around the city; that would have taken far too long. No, he rode straight towards the city gates, then went back and forth, hurling insults at the walls.

No one made a sound. Not even his mother. We all stood in perfect silence watching until Achilles rode back home with the setting sun.

Why did Priam ask me to do this? Why did he insist?

Was it to show the Greeks what he had? Was it to show Troy? Was it to show me? Remind me of what was happening?

I'm not sure. But I went every day. I stood, I watched, I listened, I felt. But I never showed what I felt. I never cried or gasped or shouted or wept. I stood alongside them and did nothing. I had no right to. And the next day, I'd do it again.

That was my war.

I never left the palace or helped with the wounded or provided any support. I was not permitted to. Another decision by someone else that has cast me as the spiteful, vain, selfish woman. The only time anyone really saw me was when I was on the walls. And I'm not sure who they really saw then.

The awful truth is that this war barely touched me.

Paris

I finally come to the crux of the matter. The reason anyone even wants to hear my story. The question of Paris. Beautiful, golden, adoring, mean, spiteful and cruel.

It's odd, as I read back over my story, I realise how my life at Sparta and Troy mirrored itself. A place, a family, a life of quiet. Yes, Troy was at war, with an army at its gates, but otherwise, it was so similar. Is that true for all women? Even during times of stress, trauma, history, the mundanity of life remains and women are at the heart of it; food cooked, clothes washed, worn holes mended, children birthed. Would a servant or noble lady of Sparta have found Troy much the same?

So now I must move on to the husband because a woman cannot be without one. The man who had Helen. Or the man that Helen had, if you listen to the storytellers. So different from Menelaus, and yet the pattern of life remained the same.

What do you want to know about Paris? About Paris and me. I've given you a taste already, but I know that's not enough. You want a proper story.

I'm not sure I'm going to give you that. Surely you can already see that I can only give you what I can. And so, that's what you'll get here as well. What I can give you. And if you need more, well, there are plenty of storytellers who can tell you those tales.

Paris. Prince of Troy. Who won the most beautiful woman in the world. Who gave up everything for love.

It's not that far off the truth really. At least, from his perspective.

The stories say that he was cast out when he was born, but that is simply not true. In the evenings and at night, when Paris would come to my rooms in between our 'worship of Aphrodite' as he called it, he would tell me stories of his life. His adventures, his deeds of derring-do, the near misses, and hilarious escapes. He was not as good a storyteller as Theseus, nor had he done as much as Menelaus, though he certainly embellished just as much, he was often full of joy. At least at the beginning.

"The story of my birth has been highly misrepresented," he'd say, a grin on his face. At times like that I'd remember why I liked him in Sparta.

He spent time as a hostage away inland from Troy, where their writing looked like birds hopping across the tablet. I suppose Paris had some brains, as he could read that script, and more than once he was asked to translate something; mostly calls for aid or polite refusals to get involved in the Greek War. He'd been sent when he was about 5 and returned when he was 11. He spent some time at sea, as it seems all Trojan men do, but mostly was kept at Troy, at his mother's side once he was back. Except for when he went out to represent his father.

Trojans in general seemed to travel much more than the Greek men; the Spartans only ever left to fight. But the Trojans seemed to leave to explore. I did like that about them. And Paris would often bring something with him to show me from his travels, or those of others. Amber from the far north, lapis lazuli from the south, spices from the east.

When I was round with our first son and feeling low, he brought me a gift. It was a wooden apple, painted a beautiful rich green gold so it glowed in the light. I thought it was just an ornament, but then he gently pressed the stalk and the side jumped out. It was a little box. I was delighted and tried it again and again. When I looked up, I found Paris watching me, not the toy, smiling. Was it my joy that made him smile, or satisfaction at his own achievement? It was always hard to tell with Paris.

I kept the apple on my vanity, and every now and then I'd find the little drawer full of something. Usually, some sweets or nuts pilfered from the kitchens, or a piece of jewellery. I always knew when something would be there, as Paris would often be lurking around, eyeing it, waiting for me to find the surprise.

In many ways that box came to symbolise his love for me. When he was happy it would overflow, but when he was sullen it would remain bare. And when he decided I was not what he wanted any more, it was gone.

I want to show you how Paris could be. Just as Menelaus was kind and cruel, so was Paris, though in a different way. He could be generous, and loving and happy and laughing. He could be overwhelming like that. During our first few years, he wouldn't stop touching me. If we were in the same room he was always near, touching my arm, my back, my leg. Even if I was at the loom, he'd find a way to touch me.

It started from our wedding night as soon as he could he latched on. I remember his leg bouncing as we sat through the feast, always wanting to get to the next thing. That night, we barely made it to the room before his hands, his lips, everything was on me. It was almost suffocating, pulling at my dress, my hair, pushing me onto the bed.

As unfair as it was, I couldn't help but compare. Paris was urgent, where Menelaus was cautious, loud where the other was quiet, expectant instead of unconcerned. By that point I knew my role, so I cooed and ahhed and pretended to shake. But I had to learn to take the initiative, I had to learn to read Paris. Menelaus gave orders, like a general, but Paris wanted more. Jocasta had told me he wanted to be adored, so I tried to do that. Even when we slept, his arms held me like a vice, keeping me close.

The war gave me some respite. Paris had to be involved. He had to attend councils, though Cassandra would say he didn't contribute much. And when he wasn't with me, he'd spend time in the training yard, battling friends who would never really hit back, or shooting arrows at nothing.

He would ask me to come and watch; at first, I would smile and demur. Menelaus never asked me to watch him train, it wasn't really the place for women. But then Paris would insist. His lips would pout, and his eyes would go cold, the sun disappearing behind a cloud. Only by doing what Paris wanted could you ensure it came out again and didn't turn into a storm.

It took me a while to really see that though. For the first year or so, he was just joy and love. When I told him I was pregnant, just a few months after we married, he was overjoyed. Truly doting. He already had children of course, but this would be different. He would bring me sweetmeats and wine, and when my belly swelled, he'd gently rub it and talk to it. Always touching.

When Bunomus was born, Paris barged into the birthing room at the sound of the first cry, desperate to see what he now had; a boy of course, a good sign.

It was a hard birth though, harder than my two at Sparta. Maybe because I was older, Troy was still strange to me, and I was surrounded by women I still didn't know. Or trust. I was scared. I'd been scared before, no one could feel that pain, feel that movement and not be. But in Troy, I could feel it hovering in the birthing room, the unspoken question.

Wouldn't it be easier if she just died?

The visceral fear that spread through my body as I crouched over the birthing bricks, feeling that tension in the room, seeing it in their eyes. I was at my most vulnerable, despite having gone through this before, maybe because I knew what was to come; how difficult, painful, and dangerous it would be. The faces of Jocasta and

Andromache in the harsh light, Cassandra prancing in the edges of my vision. For a moment, I was back in that sack, a frightened little girl. I was back in those birthing rooms in Sparta, when I lost my two nameless babies. I was back in that night when I found Paris in my room. The horror of those moments, the fear of the present, almost consuming me.

But this time, I found something to latch on to. I remember thinking one thing over and over - 'No'.

No. I refused. I would not die here, surrounded by these women, my child dead or taken away. No, no, no, no.

I don't know where that came from, where I found these words. I just know that I was so focussed on refusing death and despair and fear that it was only when I heard the cry that I realised it was over. And the chant changed to Yes.

Yes, I would live. Yes, Bunomus would live. Yes, we would survive this, Troy be damned.

The second birth at Troy was easier. I was prepared. I had my chant ready. I swear Aganus came into the world laughing, sounding just like his father.

We made such a handsome family; Bunomus had my eyes, his father's curly hair, and a tanned complexion, whereas Aganus was all Paris, golden from head to toe. If they'd grown up, I'm sure they'd have been beautiful. Paris would crow about fathering Zeus' grandsons.

I suppose we've come to it, the unavoidable. I must tell you about what happened to them. I know that many would have said I was lucky before then; I'd had two children, and both were happy and healthy, and still are. Yes, two had been lost, but they hadn't grown; we lost so many like that, the world didn't see it the same way. It was only a matter of time that what befell so many would come to my door. I've already mentioned the woman who dared to suggest that it was punishment; really, she was only the one stupid enough to say it out loud where I could hear.

So many things have happened to me in life, many painful or terrifying. But nothing like this. It's hard to say, but my story is not complete without it.

I know the storytellers tell of a collapsing roof, divine punishment, but that's not what happened. It was what takes so many babies: sickness. A plague of fever and vomiting. They were so small, only 6 and 4, and they couldn't take it. I bathed them and held them and sang to them. I tried to wipe their tears, to soothe them so the crying would stop. But then you realise that the silence is worse, that the silence means you're losing.

I even tried my mantra again, the one that had seemed to protect us all in the birthing chamber. I screamed no, no, no into the sky, at the altars, but it didn't work. It happened so quickly, I barely missed two days of my daily walk. They slipped away from me on the same night. And I couldn't scream anymore, my voice was gone, I just…went.

I remember holding them, I remember being held by Andromache, I remember the pyre we had to use because of the sickness. But I remember little else. There was a numbness. A blankness.

Sometimes I see a child, or a toy, and I feel that stab of grief, like it's happening again, and I need to remind myself that I'm no longer in that palace at Troy, and those little boys are long gone.

I think that was what finally ended Paris' love for me. I didn't see him or feel him. I was alone in my grief, but I don't know if he was. I just don't know.

I can't write more about this. I can't.

Losing the boys may have ended Paris' love for me, but it had started to cool long before that. Had started to turn into something darker, less like love. It was just small things at first. Whereas before he would touch and caress constantly, he started to give me more space. I was relieved if anything, and by then I had a routine; spaces that were mine, the children to tend to, and Paris seemed happy with that. I suppose I thought the pattern of Sparta was repeating in Troy, a comfortable calm was enveloping our family, and that's how it went; as different as the two places were, they were also the same in many ways.

Then instead of so many compliments, Paris started making suggestions. What if I wore this dress today, it suited my complexion so much better. Maybe I should fix my hair that way, it was more becoming. I should consider my posture; I was after all a princess of Troy. Perhaps I should leave the boys with the nursemaid. I should go to his practice bouts more often. I should be more exuberant. I must be more enthusiastic in bed.

It happened so gradually I barely noticed it. Until one day I woke up and I was doing whatever Paris told me. You might be thinking this doesn't sound much different to the rest of my life. Didn't I do what Menelaus told me? Didn't I always do what everyone told me? I suppose you're right. I was the good, submissive Greek girl. Trying to be what I knew I wasn't. But this was different. It felt different.

There were so many moments, big and small, that it's hard to pick one out. They merge, overcome by feeling and time. But as I look back over them, they signal to me the change that was happening, that Paris was falling out of love with me. If he'd ever been really in love with me to begin with. Perhaps, falling out of obsession is a better phrase to use.

What I remember involves me sitting at a loom, alone in my rooms. Or as alone as I ever got, surrounded by servants and slaves. Perhaps I was in the garden, a small square of earth with kitchen herbs, one of the few outdoor places I could go, and had just returned to my room. It doesn't much matter; I'm sure both scenarios happened at some point.

I was alone, and I was working at my tasks. I would always dress for my time with the ladies, for walking the walls I'd make sure I would sparkle in the sun, and I always tried my best for Paris; making myself however he wanted me to be that week. But when alone, when in my room or garden, working, I would wear something simpler. I'd still have jewellery, but otherwise, it would be the most basic dress, something that would not be ruined by children or dirt. I'm sure any woman reading this is the same. In fact, it must have been like what I'd been wearing when Paris first found me, when he was lost in Sparta.

I was dressed like this when Paris came to my rooms, flustered, agitated, looking for someone to console and caress and reassure. Or something to lash out at. And there I was. When he saw me, the colour drained from his face. He looked horrified. I was in the habit of running over to kiss him on the cheek whenever I saw him; it was expected of me. But I faltered in that moment. I thought something terrible had happened, someone had died.

But instead, he looked me up and down, and there was a look in his eye that made me pause, and then he asked in a low voice "What are you wearing?"

I was taken aback. I must have mumbled something about the work, the loom, the garden. But that was the wrong thing to say.

He exploded. His face turned pale, stark white, and he screamed at me. He screamed so his voice went hoarse. He told me I looked like a peasant, that I was an embarrassment, that I was embarrassing him, disgracing Troy. He kicked a table, and I jumped back with a yelp. He shouted at me to get changed as he stormed out, still shrieking.

The servants there had seen it all. Of, course they had, they see everything don't they? They immediately began bustling about, making sure that Paris' orders were met. I took a bath. I dressed in a fine gown, one that flattered and revealed just enough, and styled my hair as I knew Paris would like. I wore my best jewellery and scented my wrists. I was sitting at my loom, perfectly composed, when he came back. A flower appeared in front of my eyes and when I looked up, there was Paris with a penitent look on his face.

I took the flower. When I lifted it to my face, I found it had no scent.

"I'm so sorry" he said as he fell to the floor and hugged me tight. He asked me to forgive him, promised it would never happen again. And I said I did, and I knew it wouldn't. What else was I going to do?

Later, Cassandra paid one of her unexpected visits. She told me Paris had been berated and embarrassed in front of the Trojan generals that morning. I guess he took that out on me.

The days following that outburst, he was back to the way he was in the beginning. I woke up to find the apple box overflowing with jewellery.

This became a pattern; its why it's so hard for me to picture exactly what I was doing, what was happening. Rather, my memory seems to be a combination of times, of shouts, of insults, of apologies. Something would happen, usually something to do with the war; as it dragged on, everything became about the war. At least to the men. Paris would get angry, he would storm and rage at me, and then he would be calm and sweet and would be constantly touching me. I can see that now.

I tried to change to suit him, to try to avoid this anger, these moods. I would wear my finer clothes, I stopped going to the garden, I tried to always be ready for Paris.

As I said, it was after we lost the boys that he started to turn properly cold; I suppose I could forgive him that. I was cold too. Not towards him, but towards life. After that, he stopped being so conciliatory after an outburst, stopped giving presents, or even really touching me.

The real signal that something was changing was one night after we'd had sex. Paris would usually hold me close, whisper into my ear. I would have to wait until he was asleep to extricate myself from his arms so I could sleep myself. But this time, none of that. Once he had finished, he climbed off me, and sat on the bed, his head in his hands. I asked him what was wrong and reached out to him.

He lashed out at me; he didn't hit me, but he shoved my hand away with a look of disgust on his face. His words are etched into my mind – "I don't want you to touch me! Look at you! Sagging, thin and fat in all the wrong places. Cold and dead! Do you think you're worth this? What are you worth at all?"

It stung. I was still grieving, though time had passed by then. It was more that question of worth, the one that has haunted me since the day the war started. People would always speak to me about my looks, I was beautiful but there was always something that could be improved – I could always make sure I didn't smile, or cry, and my hair and skin would always receive comments. But this wasn't the same. This wasn't some stranger, whose comments might sting but didn't sink deep, who was as jealous as much as anything else. This was from my husband, the man I was trying so hard to please, who had once declared how wonderful I was. I knew my entire life, my worth as Paris had put it, relied on my looks, on the legend of my looks, and on him. Now, nearing 32, after 2 husbands, 4 children, 7 years of war, fear, pain and grief, my face was lined, there were grey strands in my hair, my stomach was rounder, my arms less toned, and my breasts sagged.

I'm sure someone else might have said I still looked lovely. People still declared me as fairest Helena, with a curvy figure, cat-like eyes, bronze skin. But we don't see the positives, do we? After years of avoiding my reflection because of the pressure of my beauty, I was now obsessed with looking for flaws and signs of failure. I had the mirrors returned to my room and poured over them, rubbing ointments and lotions onto my skin, peppering myself with anything to brighten and enhance. Though I wasn't always sure what I was failing at.

What had I had before that had caused all this, and how could I get it back? I cursed myself for not having the mirrors before, so I would be able to see what it was.

You might think me stupid, vain, easily influenced. But what else was I supposed to do? My life, my safety, everything about me, was defined by how I looked and how Paris, how Troy felt about me. As I look back, I see this panic wasn't really about my face, but about my life. That old fear creeping up on me again.

And these sentiments from Paris became more common. Starting in the privacy of the bedroom, but soon moving out to a public forum. My only real respite being that we did not spend much time together.

What made Paris spit these words? I'm not sure. It's easy sitting here now looking out across my land, to the river beyond, and to see what I hadn't noticed at the time. Or what I didn't want to notice. That he'd been slipping away from me. And I did nothing about it. I suppose I thought he would be like Menelaus; I was his wife after all. But I forgot, Paris needs to be adored. Paris needs to be the best. Paris always needs.

Add to that a war. A war that seemed like it would never end. That Paris was ill-equipped to manage. Add further two dead children, beautiful, divine boys.

It feels like it was inevitable, doesn't it?

How else could that story really end? End in the real world I mean, not in the myths or fairy tales. We all know what happens when a man becomes obsessed with a beautiful woman. Sooner or later, someone else will come along; someone more beautiful than the woman in his bed now.

I assume Paris did what men do when they are sad, but cannot show it, when they feel weak but want to be seen as strong, when they feel they have no control. They channel that into someone they see as weaker, and they look for whoever they think they deserve instead. I saw him looking at other women, of course I did, and I ignored it. I said nothing. It was natural, after all. But then, I realised he had stopped coming to my chambers completely, he stopped seeking me out altogether, and there were no new treats in my apple box.

No one said anything, no one talked about it, but it was there. Paris' attentions were moving elsewhere, and if Paris was the sun, this meant I was now in darkness. I cannot really remember how I felt about it; I felt his absence, he'd been a permanent fixture of my time at Troy. In many ways he was Troy, to me at least. With him gone, I felt alone, or I felt my aloneness. It was just me then, with my thoughts and fears.

One night, Priam did say something. There was a dinner, a feast of thanksgiving or a birthday celebration, I can't remember. Even during a war, these things continued, the sway of life. Paris was looking steadfastly at one of the serving girls.

She was very pretty; small and pert, with freckles across her face. Young.

I said something to him, I'm not sure what. Something innocuous like 'please pass the wine' but Paris was so caught up in his staring he didn't notice.

Priam did.

He stood up and the whole table fell silent. He walked around picked up the wine from Paris' side and set it down in front of me. "There you are my dear daughter. Son, perhaps you should spare a look at your lovely wife every now and again."

The table laughed. Paris blushed. He hated being singled out for jokes. He mumbled something.

"And if not, I'm sure there are plenty of men who wouldn't mind swapping! Or taking your place. What do you think of that my dear? Fancy number 3?"

There were laughs and whoops at this. At least from the men. The women, their wives, looked less thrilled. Paris went white. I'm sure I blushed and looked away.

Then Deiphobus spoke up, always happy to rattle his brother. "I'd take her off your hands brother. She was mighty fine once, I daresay that now she's a little aged but still nicely put together. I'll trade for a slave or two that I've just come into."

More laughter.

Later than night, Paris did visit my chambers, for the first time in months. He screamed and shouted. He had decided I wasn't trying my best; I wasn't beautiful or lovely, I wasn't anything. He grabbed at my breasts and arms, screaming that I was too thin here, too fat here, that I wasn't womanly anymore. Then he stormed out, and I didn't see him for days.

I think that was the moment Paris truly fell out of love with me. He'd been cold, and distant, any affection he had had been fading. But that night, in that moment, I think the last of it slipped away. There was nothing left.

I had never loved him, though I had liked him, appreciated him to an extent. I think I thought I could win him back. But I soon learned that would never happen.

When he finally returned, he was clean shaven, in some of his finest clothes, and he commanded me to dress finely too. When I was ready, I saw he had the apple box in his hands. He left and I followed in silence. He took me into one of the large antechambers and I found a line of women waiting for us. They were all young, maybe between 15 and 20, all with darker skin and curly hair. They were bound with rope and were nude.

I remember looking away confused, and I saw Deiphobus in the corner smirking. Then Paris grabbed my face and turned me to look at the women.

I remember what he said next so clearly.

"These are slaves. Purchased for their bodies. For pleasure, not position or power or prestige like a wife."

He spat the word wife and I winced; it hung in the air what I meant as a wife.

"You were so beautiful" he ran his hand over my cheek. "But even you are only human. And I want you to understand that. To understand your position. You might have my father wrapped around your finger, you might have my sister whispering my failures in your ear, you might have an army at the city gates waiting to save you. But you are not better than me. You are not the greatest beauty of all time. I am not beholden to you."

"I want you to see where you fit, and how many others just like you there are. Only so much better."

He gestured to the line of women and then approached them, peering at each one carefully.

Deiphobus came up to me and whispered in my ear. "He's looking for the best one. The closest one. He's determined to have the greatest beauty of the age. No matter who she is." He softly caressed my cheek with his finger, and I shuddered. "All in good time." I could feel the grin in his breath.

There was one towards the far end that caught Paris' attention. He stood in front of her and stared. I could see that she was staring right back. Defiant, for a slave.

Paris slit her bonds and drew her out. He was talking to her quietly. She responded and I saw Paris light up as he hadn't in a long time. As he once did with me. He pulled her with him.

As she approached, my breath caught in my throat. Standing in front of me, was me. Or a very good copy, a better version even. She was taller, leaner, darker. But otherwise, we were so similar we could be sisters. Especially the eyes. Her eyes were also green and cat-like, but with more flecks of amber in them.

She took my breath away.

Paris was smiling triumphantly. "This one will do. I'd say she's much prettier than you ever were".

I must have had a look of horror on my face because Paris flinched slightly. And then the paleness of anger came over him again. Whatever was going on inside his head, it was stirring him up.

"What did you expect? Look at you! You are not what I wanted! Not what I was promised! And you take. You take and you take, and you give nothing to me! Don't I deserve something?" He screamed and screamed, my lack of beauty, my lack of grace, my disappointment, my distance, my coldness, my dead children. "If I want to fuck a lost bastard, I'd rather have the real thing, not one with pretentions. One parading around like they're the daughter of the gods. You're not a god, Helena. You're the daughter of a whore and pimp and should never have been here."

At that I let out a cry, crumpling to the ground with tears streaming down my face.

As he watched me, his smile became cruel. "What's your name?" he asked the slave girl, who stood watching us passively. "Wait, don't say. From now on, your name is Lena, and this is for you." He gave her my apple box.

That was especially cruel. He knew that's the name Nest had given me, I had told him that, in one of those rare moments I'd share something with him. He had even used it himself on occasion, only in the most intimate moments; as we lay together, as we held our sons for the first time. And then he took it. He took it and gave it to this 'new' me, the real beauty he wanted so much. It was like I was wiped out. It hurt me, it scared me, and as I lost my name and my gift, I realised I had lost Paris.

What had been going on in Paris' head?

I'm not sure, and now I'll never know. Someone might look at the glory of Hector and wonder if that propelled him. Or consider his time spent away from his family as a child. Or the way his mother doted on him, his father ignored him, the glories that so many other kings around him won. Whatever it was, it's what drove him to come for me and it's what drove him away.

I never loved Paris. I had not come to Troy because I wanted to. But everyone likes being wanted. I had assumed his love for me would hold, and I'd been flattered, believed in my own power, even as I'd told Cassandra that it was fleeting.

Because whilst taking a woman that looked like me and giving her my name was painful enough, he then installed her in my rooms as my companion. Someone I had to look at every day, spend every day with, and watch every night as she was summoned to Paris' rooms. It was painful. Watching her, seeing her in the gifts Paris would give her. Hearing him whisper to her when he came ostensibly to see me. Seeing my first few years with him repeated, the time when I had someone who wanted me, and my children.

No one at Troy did or said anything. What was there to say?

It was in those days afterwards, as I saw Paris flutter about her as he once had me, that I think I began to examine myself. I finally removed those mirrors and threw away the ointments and cosmetics that I thought would make me right, make me beautiful again. I realised finally, that I was truly alone at Troy, and whilst that meant I had lost my husband and my children, it also meant that I was now free to…to what? To be me? Or to figure out who I was? To be someone other than Helena of Troy?

In a terrible way, I should thank Paris for his cruelty. I should say a prayer and pour some wine in remembrance of that. Without his actions, my life would have been very different. He set the pieces in place for the future, and he gave me the time, the ability to start thinking properly. Just as Cassandra said I should.

Of course, I still had a role to play, even though I was Paris' wife only in name. I still walked those walls every day and stood facing out. Once Hector was gone, it fell to Paris to play the hero, though we all knew he couldn't do it.

There is a famous story from near the end of the war. Paris marched out to meet Achilles in combat. I was on the wall watching, as I should be. Lena was elsewhere, I'm not sure why. Paris would never be a match for Achilles. Even far away, with dust clouding our view, we could see that. Paris didn't have the skill, the strength, or the determination. In the stories they tell, Paris is whipped away by Aphrodite and into the arms of Helen.

But the truth is more mundane. There was a dust cloud, it was windy that day and the barren earth between Troy and the camp was liable to blow up plumes. When that dust cloud blew up, obscuring everything, Paris, who had been on his back, scuttled on his knees back to Troy. And he went straight to the arms of this new Lena, who I'm sure told him everything he needed to hear.

It was this Lena who tended to Paris before he died.

Again, the songs are all wrong. They say he died from an arrow, fighting the Greeks while they overran the city. That never happened.

Paris wanted to prove his worth, to make up for running away from Achilles. He wanted so badly to be the great soldier. He gathered a group of trusted friends and went out to the Greek camps at night. I understand there were many of these raids, from both sides, each eking out small victories and defeats whilst everything else stood still.

From what I've been told, he was successful, creating one of those moments where it seemed that Troy might break the Greeks. It's why the final plot by Odysseus worked so well, that hope grew inside the walls of the city. But it never happened. Someone, a figure in the dark, maybe a boy with a bow, shot him through the stomach. He only made it back to the city because of his horse. Everyone else in the party survived.

Stomach wounds are always bad, so I'm told. You could hear the screaming throughout the palace as the surgeon worked on him. Then came the infection. Paris lingered for days, a harsh contrast to the fever that carried away my boys. The smell from his room was awful, and only Jocasta seemed able to spend any time there. Priam never went near it; I don't think he could. Hector's loss had destroyed him, and the death of Paris was burning and salting the ground. Even if Troy won now, who would rule?

Paris asked for someone. But who was unclear. Did he say Helen or Helena or Lena? Or maybe it was another name? Someone else to give comfort.

This caused great confusion. As we stood outside the sickroom, I insisted he must mean his new Lena, and she, when asked directly, demurred to me as his wife. Eventually, Jocasta shoved us both inside.

The fever had set in by then. Despite what the doctor did, Paris was delirious. He made no sense. He was rambling. Sending us both in together was probably a mistake. He kept looking between us, confused.

At one point, he grabbed my hand, and squeezed it so tightly it hurt. His clouded eyes looked at mine filled with sorrow. Then he let out a cry of pain falling back and writhing. I fetched a cup of water, and when I returned, he had hold of Lena's hand, pressed to his lips, saying how much he loved her, how beautiful she always would be, and how sorry he was for everything that happened.

Did he think she was me? Maybe. Was he sorry for all he'd done or just for himself? We'll never know.

Lena looked terrified, pale despite her dark skin. She retreated, shrunk away from Paris, as I bought the cup to his lips, but Paris wouldn't let go. He knocked the cup from my hand and ordered her back. She dutifully followed, but I could see how much she didn't want to be in the room.

I moved to her, took her other hand in my own, and told her I could take over. As I stood there, I saw Paris' eyes widen in fright and wonder. It was as she was gently passing his hand to me that Paris convulsed; he went rigid and started foaming at the mouth.

We both screamed and I was at the door when the doctor came in. I know I was babbling; it was hard to stay calm. At that moment, the doctor ushered me out of the room, calling another to give me some potion. No doubt he felt that as the wife, I was in danger of becoming hysterical. As I was removed, I saw her still in there, the doctor shouting orders for her to follow.

I left her with him. She didn't want to be there, and I left her there. I wonder now what she saw on that bed. Was it Paris, or was she reliving another night, another sickroom? I think of how my own horrors come back upon me, cause me to freeze and cry, and I wonder if she had her own horrors made manifest in that room. And I left her there.

When I woke up, it was all over. Lena was sitting in my room; her gown was soaked and smeared, her face was ashen, her eyes red. All she could say was, "He's gone."

That was the end of Paris, prince of Troy. We never got the chance to bury him. He was in the cold storage when the Greeks came. I assume the body burned with everything else.

Lena and Deiphobus

I think I might have surprised you. Created a new question that you might want to ask. Or a new set of questions.

Who was this other Lena? What was she to me? How does she fit into my story?

In some of the tales they tell of the fall of Ilium, they sometimes mention a daughter, born to Paris and me, called Helen. I think they've gotten confused, as they have on so many topics, and it's this Lena they refer to. She was very far from being a daughter, but she was there. The other Lena of Troy, perhaps the true Helen of Troy.

She was a slave, a servant, a concubine. I was a queen, a wife, a mother.

Were we really that different?

I admit I was cold to her after Paris selected her and installed her in my rooms. I commanded her, more harshly than I'd ever commanded Menelaus' women. I would order her to do the most menial tasks, the chamber pots and menstruation rags. She was not supposed to do that, she was installed as a slave, a companion for me; another trick played by Paris. But he did nothing to stop me, which left her scrubbing out piss-stained clothes whilst wearing jewellery finer than my own.

That was something I noticed about her; she also wore a lot of jewellery. Just like me.

The similarity between us in general was striking, though on closer inspection there were differences, other than just youth. The ways in which we both stood, the texture of our skin – with her callused palms against my own smooth hands – and our hair, her curls were tighter, an explosion away from her head, whereas mine were looser than that. And yet, we were close enough to make me wonder.

How long was I like this? It's difficult to say. Time is a funny thing, especially when suspended in anger or jealousy or powerlessness. It's easy to see now how those things drove me, as they did with so many of those under me. When I took any notice them; I can't really recall the faces any of the servants and slaves that surrounded me in Troy or Sparta. Except those who slept with my husbands.

You'd think I'd be kinder. That I'd understand none of this was her doing, or that I'd be more sensitive, even protective, of the slaves that surrounded me. But I wasn't. I didn't see them, only myself. They were a part of life; it was the way it was, just like my role as a wife commanded by her husband. It's hard to hear, it's hard to admit as I want to be the good person, the hero of my story. But it's the truth. And if I can't admit it now, when will I?

So how did she take it? How did she handle this cruel mistress? The way all slaves do, in silence and with impeccable manners. The rage and grief she must have felt and kept hidden away is unimaginable.

However long it was, eventually it had to break. Just as it's hard to stay terrified, it's hard to stay angry. Especially when you have little else to hold on to. So, I started to talk to her.

Her Greek was very good. Surprisingly good. I wasn't sure what to say at first, the most obvious opening question was also a painful one, but I asked it anyway.

"What is your name?"

I remember she arched her eyebrow at that. A perfect curve above her eyes and her high cheekbones. She was judging the question and judging me; trying to figure out what I was up to.

"Why do you want to know?"

I knew I had to choose my words carefully, so I shrugged and said, "Because I'd like to."

"My name is Lena," she said, looking away from me, disappointed. "That is all that matters now."

"And before you were Lena?" I asked. I'm not sure, but I think my voice cracked then.

"I was someone else." Her gaze returned to me, inscrutable. "I was from somewhere far, far away from here."

I had to look away, but I could feel her studying me, examining me, just as I had done to her.

"I am from beyond Egypt," she said carefully, "my brother sold me when I was young to traders who brought me across the desert, so I came to be here."

That caught my attention, and the question was out of my mouth before I could stop myself. "Your people trade as far as Troy? Travel to the cities?"

What did I hope she'd tell me? Now I'm older, I find I don't care as much about my origin, but then? The possibility of a glimpse into where I came from was enticing, even though I had no real ability to form the words, to ask the questions. I still didn't really know what I wanted. In that moment though, I felt like I was on the edge of something.

She nodded. "They do. They spend time with your people." Dancing around the question, she was good at that.

"And what of your home?" I wanted to draw her out, I wanted to know about the lands away from Troy.

But I saw her eyes harden, a barrier went up to block whatever had opened between us.

"This is my home."

She could not be enticed to say more, no matter how I pressed her. Occasionally something would slip; the name of a fruit, the mention of an animal, and she had a small, strange amulet I'd sometimes hear her muttering over, as if in prayer. But there were never details, any real information was just out of reach. I think now she came from Kush, but she could have come from beyond there. I'll never know.

Maybe I should have asked more, but we all choose to tell our story, and when and to whom, as I am proving right now.

Besides, for all these questions, for all our similarities and differences, hadn't we both ended up at the same place, with the same man, with the same name? Me as a queen, her as a slave.

After that, I was happier to have her with me. I'm not sure we became friends – could we ever? But we were companions; we spent time together, we spoke to each other. We spoke about nothing really; how the plants were doing, the weather, how good the meat was today, and idle gossip. She would accompany me on my daily excursions to the walls. And when I cried on my babies' birthdays, she held me. She was a comfort to me. And I think I was one to her as well.

Lena was beautiful and clever, and so much stronger than me. I think she saw the world clearly. And she saw me perfectly.

And what of her and Paris? It always felt like she was waiting for something, like she was always ready for when an opportunity presented itself. I really can't blame her, and I think she saw Paris as such an opportunity. I didn't see them together often, at least, not after those first few weeks, but when I did, she would be looking up at him in adoration. She would caress him and whisper in his ear and giggle. Doing all the things I never did right, that I had to be cajoled and reminded to do. The new Lena was much better at this that I was. She never gave Paris children though, and I always wondered about that.

When I think back to Lena, I think of the things we never spoke about, like Paris and her history, and mine. Part of me wishes we had. But perhaps it was for the best.

I never saw her cry or shout, or be anything but serene, except with Paris of course. And when he died. She cried out as I did when we saw him, and she was in shock when he was gone. Both of us consumed by questions.

What would happen to us with Paris gone? Without him, what were we?

My position was safer than hers, and we both knew that; a war was being fought for me.

She was a mess, her face tear streaked with smudged eyes and lips, and her clothes were covered in blood and other fluids. It took two of us to get her to the bath. We cleaned her, dressed her, and put her to bed.

While she was asleep, Cassandra came to me; she looked perfectly fine. Neat and proper as usual. You'd never know she'd lost another brother.

"We aren't going to tell anyone," she said quietly, and in my memory, I swear I can see a smile on her face; she always did love a secret. "We're not telling anyone until things are sorted. It'd be bad for morale."

She didn't say what she meant by 'things are sorted', but I could read between the lines; she meant me, the war, the only things that really occupied Troy then. As his wife though, I knew I had a duty.

"What about his body? What about the funeral?"

Cassandra raised an eyebrow at me. "Caring now, are we?" It was snide. "He'll be placed in the cold storage."

I nodded. What could I do? I looked at the other Lena, asleep in my bed. She looked hollow and too young for all this.

Cassandra stayed hovering "Aren't you going to ask about you?"

"What about me?" I felt tired. A hundred years old, with the weight of so many deaths on my hands. I wasn't sure what mattered.

"They're discussing it." I didn't ask who 'they' were; it might have been Priam, but he was already broken by the death of Hector, I couldn't imagine how he would be with Paris. When I saw him the next day, on my walk across the walls, he was tiny, diminished, and his eyes were glazed. He only moved with help from Jocasta. I never saw him again after that.

"Don't worry. There's a plan in place. There's always been a plan in place."

Of course, there would be, how could there not? I felt disappointment flow through me. I hadn't even realised that I'd had a tiny flame of hope, hope that I would be left alone or could be let go in some way. But that was doused out, because of course there were contingencies for contingencies.

"And what about Lena?" Cassandra looked confused, then she understood. "You mean the whore? What about her? We'll sell her on I suppose, there's sure to be a buyer one way or another."

"You can't…" I began, but she cut me off.

"You're right, we can't. It'll be hard to do anything with her in the palace and selling outside will raise suspicions."

"I'll keep her." I said. I hadn't really thought about it.

Cassandra opened her mouth to say something, but clearly decided against it. A rarity. She just nodded.

Later, when Lena woke, I was there beside her. She looked groggy. Her beauty gone for the moment in her pale and wasted face. I tried to tell her what was happening, and that I would keep her.

This got her attention. She sat up straight, became rigid. After a moment she nodded. "Yes mistress," was all she said.

I had thought I was helping, but maybe I wasn't. Of course, if things had gone differently, I might have had the chance to make it up to her.

As it was, in less than a month, the Greeks would be in the palace.

As it turned out, Deiphobus was the plan Cassandra had alluded to. Priam is said to have had many sons, but with Jocasta, it was only three, so only those three mattered. If anything happened to Paris, Deiphobus would be the next in line. I'm sure it wasn't quite as simple as that; whilst Priam lived there would be advisors vying for power, and there was Hector's son. But Deiphobus was an adult, he had been blooded in the war, and he was there. From the moment I had arrived, it had been agreed that should my husband fall, Deiphobus would be next in line.

I wondered afterwards if they already had husbands four and five lined up as well, just in case.

The secret of Paris' death made marrying Deiphobus difficult, but no more so than my still living husband, out on the battlefield.

I haven't spoken much about Deiphobus in these pages; he's been at the edges, lurking, smirking. A reflection of how I saw him. If Paris was in Hector's shadow, then Deiphobus was covered in darkness; the third son, not as skilled as Hector, or charming as Paris, or loved as Cassandra. But he was there. I daresay he was quite clever and handsome in his own way, but not as much as his siblings. He doesn't even seem to have made it into some of the stories of Troy, so I'm not alone in ignoring him.

He would whisper strange things to me when I passed him, would catch a sliver of my dress, or gently lay a finger on my arm. I would try to avoid him, and knowing I was going to marry him filled me with dread in a way the others hadn't.

I'd had no choice but to marry both Menelaus and Paris; the situations demanded it. I had wanted to marry Menelaus, in the way I wanted to grow up and marry, and I would have married whomever my father chose. I had wanted to marry Paris to protect myself, as I needed to do. But this was different. My choice was gone completely, I didn't like Deiphobus, I didn't want to be near him, and the idea of having sex with him in my bed made me feel sick.

I know I've written it before, but I want to be clear; I have never felt that spark, that attraction, that desire that others talk of. I didn't enjoy sex, but I understood I had to take part. But I had enjoyed contact, usually what came afterwards. I had accepted it, and with Menelaus and Paris, I did what I had to. But with Deiphobus, the idea of his touch revolted me.

But I had no choice. Troy had no choice. They couldn't let me go. And Deiphobus was now poised to be king. Priam was failing, and there was no other option.

Deiphobus came to see me a few days after Paris had died. He wanted to talk to me about the wedding. He wanted a secret one, as soon as possible, before his brother's funeral.

“But I know you’re not bothered with convention when it comes to marriage anyway,” he said, sitting close and gently running his finger down my arm.

I know I shivered. I don’t know what he thought that resulted from, but it made him smile.

“And if we’re already breaking convention…” he leaned in, grabbed my head, and kissed me. It was cold and sloppy, and I felt myself gagging. His hand was clawing at my breasts, at my dress. I wiggled against him but that just encouraged him. I did the only thing I could think of, I reached out, grabbed his groin and squeezed as hard as I could.

He broke away with a shriek and started screaming incoherently. He raised his hand, but a loud clatter sounded out before he could bring it down.

We both turned to see Lena, a bowl and jug on the floor, her hem spattered with water and flower petals.

She started apologising, for interrupting, making a mess, and called for someone to help with the clean-up. It was masterful, the way she managed to make it seem like she was trying not to interrupt, and then filled the room with people. Finally, she reminded me of our plans for the garden that day.

Deiphobus was scowling the entire time, but he had the grace to leave politely. Kissing my hand as he went. He left a smear of saliva on it, and as soon as he was gone, I was scrubbing it vigorously.

As Lena and I walked to the garden I tried to talk about it. Lena faced me, a sharp look in her eye.

“This is what we have to do” was all she said.

It reminded me of the words of Jocasta when I first came to Troy: *"this is the way of the world"*.

"Haven't I already done it enough?" I remember asking. There were tears in my eyes, but I could feel anger, not sorrow bubbling in my chest.

Lena gently brushed my hair from my face. "No woman will ever have done it enough."

She was right. There may even be women reading this who feel no sympathy, and looking back, how ignorant of me to speak these words to Lena, who was more trapped that I have ever been. They say a gilded cage is still a cage, but those people do not understand the importance of gilt.

The next few days were a blur as I absorbed this, as I understood what the rest of my life would involve. Being passed from man to man, until I was no longer considered of use. And once I was old, once no one saw beauty in me any longer, or I could no longer bear children, what then?

I couldn't let it happen. Whether it was here or in Sparta or somewhere else completely, I just could not let my life continue like this. But I had no idea how I could prevent it. Run away from Troy? With the Greek army on our doorstep? With Deiphobus already planning what would happen next? And besides, I didn't know how; how to run, how to live. The palace was safer for me.

There was another way of course. I would be lying if I said I didn't eye the knives that would lie around me, the potions. But I wasn't sure. And to take that path, you must be sure.

Perhaps Deiphobus sensed my thoughts because I was moved. A different set of rooms, closer to his, on the other side of the palace. More open, better views, bigger. I did wonder who they had belonged to before. When I found a dress that once belonged to Andromache, I knew. Perhaps Deiphobus wanted the best room, wanted to emulate Hector. He didn't seem to realise how unpleasant it was, stealing a dead man's bed, when his wife was wailing in his tomb.

I was puzzling over all this, dreading the moment Deiphobus would appear at my bed, wishing I could talk more with Lena, for anyone who might listen, and then the inevitable happened.

The war ended.

The Fall of Helena

They say you do not see a battle. You hear it, smell it, feel it.

Maybe from that perspective, my whole life has been a battle.

I was asleep, along with most of the city, when the Greeks slipped out of their horse.

You probably thought I was going to dispel that part of the story. Tell you that's a load of horseshit, and that there was a much more practical way into the city. A drain perhaps? A hole in the wall?

I'm sorry to disappoint you. It is completely true.

Everyone knows what happened – it's the best part of the story. The crafty Greeks pretended to give up. They hid their ships, built a large model horse, and used it as a peace offering, honouring Athena. Which Priam, heartbroken and sick, accepted. In the palace there was a feeling of relief, though I knew this had sealed my fate with Deiphobus.

I remember my heart sinking at that. I knew I needed to think of something, a way to escape him. But that could wait until the morning. The rest of Troy wanted to celebrate.

I'm not sure how many men were enclosed inside that horse, or who they were; I only saw it from afar, saw the commotion Cassandra made. I'd guess it could have held 20 men at most. But that's all they needed. And when you remember that most of Troy had celebrated well into the night, it made the plan even easier.

It wasn't the noise though, that woke me that night. It was the smell. It had been hot, painfully so all week, and I had left all the shutters open to draw in the breeze. My new chambers were closer to the street, facing the outer court, so there was more chance of a breath of wind. And the noise of the revellers had helped me doze off.

The smoke that drifted through in the early hours was acrid. I don't know what they'd set fire to, but it was what woke me. Once I was awake, I could hear the screams and shouts, the clashing and clanging. I could feel the earth shaking as thousands of Greeks ran through the city, and thousands of Trojans ran away from them.

I knew what was happening. In that moment, I felt relief for myself. It was over. I suppose I should have felt fear, but I was tired. Everyone was. Knowing the war had truly ended was like releasing a deep breath. Though it did not last. The screams came closer, I started to see people running through the courtyard, and that's when it struck me. They'd be coming for me.

This thought drove me forward; I remember I was concerned about what I should wear. It sounds ridiculous, I know. But if there was one certainty, it was that someone was going to come and find me. It wasn't a question of who, but of who first. And what image did I want to project?

I went for simple but quality. I adorned myself in jewellery, my trusted swan brooch at my shoulder. I ignored the make-up box, but pinned my hair up in an elegant style, sparkling with gold and gems, leaving it uncovered. It sounds strange, but I felt like I was waking up. Perhaps this was the point the worst of my grief, for the war, for Paris, for my children, left me? Perhaps it was just the relief? Perhaps it was a new me; the person I'd been turning into over the past 9 years.

I could hear the panic in the palace. Furniture was being toppled, vases shattered, feet slapping against the floor, and out of the window I saw people running with their arms full. Many of them loyal Trojans. I couldn't blame them, running was their only option, and if they got away, they'd need something to start a new life.

I decided to stay by the window. The sun was rising, and the sky was a beautiful riot of colour - reds, purples, yellows, and that light shimmering blue. More than that, I wanted to see what was happening. It was my only way to get an idea of who might come. Because I knew they would.

I had moved a couch to the window when I heard movement behind me.

It was Lena. She looked stunning. Wearing rich jewel colours that brought out her eyes. themselves heavily lined in kohl, her lips painted a stunning red, and her hair unstyled, flowing beautifully around her face.

I found that any lingering jealousy or anger or spite I felt towards her was gone completely.

Silently, she came to join me on the couch. This younger, fairer, better version of myself. As we watched, I gently took her hand in mine. She gave me a slight squeeze and we sat there, watching, and waiting. She surprised me, as we sat together, waiting to see what the fates had in store. She took a deep breath and muttered softly, "My name is Amaros. I want someone to know."

She thought she was going to die, here, next to me.

I said nothing. I smiled weakly and squeezed her hand in return.

No one else came to my room. None of the servants. None of the ladies of court or the royal ladies of Troy. None of the men. If Paris had been alive, would he have come? Maybe. But certainly not Deiphobus. I doubt he went to look for any of us.

I don't blame them for that. They had no loyalty to me, nor I to them. And now the end was here, they wouldn't want to be associated with me. They had their own decisions to make; live and be taken, try to flee into the unknown, drink poison and die on their own terms.

It's funny, but the idea of drinking poison, or slashing my wrists did not occur to me in that moment. And it clearly didn't occur to Lena either. Just days earlier, it had flitted across my mind, but now, it wasn't a choice I would even consider. Perhaps the Fates were already at work.

The sun had fully risen by the time we saw Greek soldiers begin to flood into the courtyard.

It was nearly time.

Soon enough, we heard the clanging sounds as people came closer to my room, and the door burst open.

I took a deep breath, righted my clothes, and stood to face the two soldiers. Lena at my side.

To call these boys soldiers was laughable. They looked barely old enough to shave, made worse by the armour that did not fit them and swords that were rusted and dented, the remnants of older, dead men.

They looked shocked. By this point, I imagine most of the palace was empty, ransacked, so finding anyone was a surprise. But finding me! I was the reason they were there, after all. At least in theory.

I'm sure they had a description, and there were few others who would be in such splendid rooms in the royal chambers of the palace. No doubt they had crowed about how they would be the ones to find Helena, to bring her to heel. But they'd never actually expected to do so.

"Helena of Sparta?" one of them asked, his voice shaking and his eyes darting to Lena.

I had stepped forward when my name was said, but the boys had not even noticed. Their eyes seemed to slide over me, away from me; they only had eyes for her. Both were staring at Lena, giving her short and shaking bows.

And it dawned on me.

These two boys, who had barely been old enough to lift a sword when I left Sparta, had no idea what I looked like.

They had a description, a concept, a dream, a legend. They had an idea of the most beautiful woman in the world. Divinely created. Desirable to any man. A woman who could drive nations to war. An idea that would appeal to them.

What would such a woman look like to these boys? What did they dream about at night? Was it a 35-year-old who had birthed half a dozen children and lost all of them? Whose eyes and brow were crinkled from crying? Whose hair had streaks of grey at the temple? Who was dressed richly, but plainly? Who showed a bare face?

Or was it the woman beside me? Who was young and beautiful? Who had dark skin and curled hair? Who wore fine clothes, jewellery, and a fierce expression? Whose description so matched what my own had once been?

Which of us had a face that could launch a thousand ships?

I almost laughed. It was so funny. The myth of me growing so far beyond what I was, or what I could be. In the palace, I had been kept away from what was happening, with only Cassandra telling me what she would find amusing for me to know. I had not thought about it, but standing there, looking at those two boys, it was clear; I'd become so much more than a woman. And I, me, would never live up to that ideal.

I think Lena saw all this too; the way she looked at me, moved almost to mirror me. I could almost see her trying to decide the best thing to do. To see if this was the moment she'd been waiting for, for something better than she had.

But as we stood in that strange tableau, waiting for someone to make a decision, there was a loud clatter as the door burst open. I could tell from his armour and stance this was an older warrior. And it was familiar. I knew who it was before he took off his helmet.

"Menelaus," I whispered. I couldn't really believe it. After so long, here he was. My husband. He must have run through the city, straight to the palace, ignoring the soldiers and people around him. Straight here, to find me.

He had also grown older, but it seemed now he was diminished; not the strong, overpowering man I'd known. He was thin, not lean, or muscular, he was limping heavily, with his once greying hair now pure white, and his face was like leather. Even his eyes looked different; no longer holding the quiet confidence and power of a hero, but the wild and sad look of the defeated. Even as his army conquered the city.

He looked stunned to see me. I can only imagine what he was feeling – anger, hope, shock. Perhaps he had never expected to find me? Or this scene was already so far from his fantasies, he didn't know what to do next?

We were stuck like that, the two of us, for long moments. Just looking at each other. Amazed this time had come. I'm sure we both were certain we'd never see each other again.

The spell was broken by the young soldiers. "What do you want us to do with her, sir?"

Menelaus looked physically shaken. "Leave," he whispered harshly.

As the boy soldiers slowly backed out, I grabbed Lena's hand, and she squeezed my arm, letting me know she'd stay by my side. Menelaus saw this, seemed to accept it.

"Helena" his voice was harsh, but I could hear the emotion in it. "Oh Helena" I thought he might come for me, strangle me as he almost had all those years ago. He might not have looked as imposing as he once had, but even a defeated man is dangerous – sometimes the most dangerous. But instead, he crumpled; he fell to his knees, tears in his eyes.

"What am I to do?" he wailed. It wasn't a question for me. It was to the gods. It was to them he raised his head and arms and bellowed like a calf being slaughtered.

"I should run you through. Adulterer! Betrayer! I should take my sword and run it through your belly and show the world your naked body. Strip you bare!"

I felt Lena tense beside me. His voice was full of hate at that moment. But finally, I felt my voice bubbling up.

You already know that I am not one for speaking up, that all my life things have happened to me, around me. It's something Cassandra herself told me, in one of her more perceptive moments. I am not brave, or strong, or powerful. But you don't always have to be. So often, we speak of strength or bravery as being a continuous trait, but they're not. You just must have courage when it matters. Like I did with Priam. Like I did in that moment before Menelaus.

"Then do it. Kill me. Parade me. Take me home. Let my children see me dead. And put me to rest. If that is what you want?" the calmness of my voice surprised me. I have always remained serene.

"What else can I do? You have made this happen!" Menelaus was shouting; I'd never seen him like this. His anger had always been silent.

“I did not make this happen! You, and Paris, and Odysseus and all the others made this happen.”

“And what happens next is also up to me,” he hissed, echoing the words Priam had uttered that fateful day 9 years ago.

Menelaus lurched upwards, still nimble, and slammed into me, pinning me to the wall. My head missed the torch bracket by a finger width, but I could feel the heat from the flames on my face. Lena stood close, silent but watchful and tense, as he brought his sword to my throat.

I was surprised, but still felt that calm courage. I looked him in the eyes. I wanted him to see me as he took my life. But then Lena pounced; she grabbed his arm and pulled. She couldn’t do much but managed take him by surprise. He loosened his grip enough that I was able to wiggle out.

The three of us stood there, quiet, staring at each other.

“What else is there?” Menelaus mumbled to himself. “Bring you home as my wife? Go back to what we were? We cannot. I cannot. Can I?”

He looked at me as if to ask permission. He’d never asked me for anything before. For a moment, I almost said yes, consent without desire. The pull of my children, my sisters, my childhood, was strong, and it crashed over me in a wave. I think if I’d said yes in that moment, if I’d gone to him then, he would’ve taken me with him.

But that sliver of courage remained. I was doing what Cassandra had told me to do - think.

When I had thought I would marry Deiphobus, I had felt the need to escape, and that same feeling came to me now. Pushing away the other concerns, the other calls to return to

Sparta. I could see clearly how my life would repeat, the same as before, in both Sparta and Troy; home, people, husband, chores, children, until I died. I thought I'd spent 9 years as a prisoner, but hadn't it been longer? It made my head spin. I needed something to ground me.

I looked over at Lena.

The slave that looked so like me, whose life had been so different, and yet who had ended up in this room, at this moment. Just like me. And I wondered. She looked back. I'll never know what she was really thinking, but she was cleverer and stronger than me; she had been waiting for more, for something to change her life and she knew what I had been wondering for the past few months. Understanding passed between us, a silent agreement about what would happen next, built upon the years we had spent together; as rivals, as companions, as mourners, as women trapped and without a choice. This moment gave us both a choice, one neither of us could have dreamt of. If we wanted to take it. If we were both brave enough to take it.

Lena nodded her head in assent, and I nodded back. We had each chosen a new path; or perhaps the path remained the same, it was just the walker who was changing? It's easy to twist together two similar balls of yarn.

I turned to Menelaus, ready to answer.

"You can have your wife, your queen," I said slowly, carefully, not wanting to rouse him again. "But not me."

"You do not want to kill me. But you do not want a wife that betrayed you. What if you take back a new wife? One to be your new Queen? One that can live up to the stories that have come about. A new Helena."

Menelaus looked confused, even as Lena drew closer to me.

"Do you think Agamemnon, Odysseus, or any of your men will look at me and see a woman worth fighting for? Am I the Helena you remember?" I asked. "What do you think they will do? Dead or alive, will they want me?"

It felt liberating to say it out loud, finally.

"What do you mean?" Menelaus looked tired, but I could see that he was taking me in. Really looking at me as I was, not letting his rage cloud him. He saw me, and I could that he understood. Neither of us were the stuff of legend anymore, if we ever had been.

"You take me instead," Lena's accent was almost gone, she sounded mostly Trojan. I could see Menelaus bristle at her impertinence, but his eyes roamed her body. I could almost see him thinking of how she could be his. This new woman. This beautiful creature. He had always liked beautiful women.

"Doesn't she look like me? Better than me? Doesn't she look like the most beautiful woman in the world?"

"But she's not you?" His expression did not match his question; I could see he was drawn into this.

"You've done this before. For Agamemnon and the throne that should have been yours," I paused, I knew I was treading on dangerous ground. "No one will know. And anyone who thinks it won't dare to say it," I whispered. I wondered if Cassandra would be happy with me now. "You need a Helena, Menelaus, you need a beautiful woman to be a symbol of victory."

"And I would make a much better Queen that her," Lena said, and I almost smiled. Of course she would.

Menelaus was considering this, and I knew he was already thinking of how he could have us both. "But you'll still be around? Where will you go? Someone will recognise you and rumours will start. Don't you see yourself Helen? You are older, but you are still lovely."

He lifted his hand and gently brushed my cheek. I could feel the tears. I had never realised how much I didn't want this. How much I didn't want to be a Queen or be beautiful or have this life. I was so close.

I turned away. I knew what I had to do.

"The woman you leave this palace with needs to be beautiful, no matter if she's dead or alive." It was a statement. Both Lena and Menelaus nodded looking puzzled.

I grabbed the glowing brazier and shoved it into my face.

Leaving Troy

The pain was unimaginable, though in my memory it came later.

At first, I just felt the heat. I could smell the fire burning my hair, singeing my clothing. I faintly heard the yelps of the other two as they pulled my arms away from my face, the brazier falling to the floor, spent.

I was screaming. I know that much, but the rest is faint. I remember grabbing hold of Menelaus shrieking, "now you have no choice," as he held me and sobbed.

We stayed like that for a while. Or perhaps it was just a moment. It's not clear in my head. When I think about it, my scars twinge, and I flush hot.

I know I must have been in pain. In shock. But I do remember Menelaus' tears and his arms around me. Whether he was crying for me or himself, I don't know.

I know it was Lena who placed something soothing over my face and head. Or should I call her Helena from now on?

Who else could it have been? I'm sure she knew how to treat burns. I'm sure she knew how to treat a lot of things. And I know that she took charge, as I never could. I recall her whispering to Menelaus. Her grasping his hand. In my mind she even slaps him, though I'm not sure that can be true.

I remember vaguely thinking that these two made a fine couple.

She became of Helena of Troy, or Helen as they say. The true Helen that the stories talk about. The one who returned with Menelaus to Sparta, had children, mourned the dead, and continued to inspire men throughout the Greek cities.

And I? I didn't know who I was.

The next thing I remember is the pain of being moved. I'll never know exactly what happened. But I was on a make-shift stretcher being carried through the palace. It was two young boys who carried me. I'm not sure what they thought. I was dazed. My face was burning, but my body was frozen, and I had to keep my head to one side to let the bile dribble from my mouth.

At some point we were outside.

It was still a beautiful day. Shining sun. Gentle breeze. I saw a tree in full bloom and was struck by how lovely it was. Even in my pain and incoherence, I remember that tree. I see it with perfect clarity; it was everything a tree in summer should be. Being carried beneath I watched as a soft white petal was picked up by the wind and drifted down to me. I felt so far away and at peace.

But all you could hear were screams. It was like the entire city was screaming. The air was filled with smoke, and the boys carrying me slipped on the blood that covered the streets. As they slid, jolting me, I came to my senses, realising I couldn't drift away. And with that, the horror of what was around me, of what I had done to myself finally dawned on me.

I knew they'd be heading towards the harbour. Or somewhere with ships. As we moved, we came across more people, fleeing just like us. Even others carrying stretchers. It was hard to tell how many there were, whether they were small groups or individuals, or how those two mixed and mingled and changed as people ran; some abandoning loved ones, others helping people they'd never met.

Why did these boys carry me? I have no idea; I suppose Lena or Menelaus paid them. They saved my life, but I have no idea who they were, Greek or Trojan. Once we reached the sea, they clearly thought their job was done, as they dropped me and left.

I could smell the ocean, and I could hear the ships. I could see the others being left around me; the dying who couldn't make it. Who wouldn't make it.

I felt a surge of anger then. That I had done this to myself, and I wasn't going to survive. I didn't know I had the strength to survive, but I lunged up screaming. Half a dozen people around me jumped back; it probably looked like the dead waking.

I grabbed one of them, a middle-aged woman, and I hissed at her to take me to the boat. I can't really recall her face now, she had grey, curled hair, and a sturdy figure.

She tried to uncurl my fingers from her arm, so I sank my broken nails in deeper. "You can have these" I said, shoving my left arm at her, covered as usual with golden bracelets and rings.

Greed is a great motivator, and she was a quick thinker, she understood. As she gazed at the rest of me, she must have realised there was opportunity here; if I died, she could take it all. Even if I didn't, she might still be able to. So, she took me gently under the arms, and forced a pathway onto one of the ships.

I don't know how long it was before we set sail. I was lowered into the hold with the other injured, and we were crammed together with little light. Eventually, I felt the movement of the ship. It reminded me briefly of the one I'd come to Troy in. But then I'd been in a royal craft, with space, good food, and the knowledge of what was happening, where I was going – unsure of the future, but certain of the general points. This ship was stuffed to overflowing with people; scared, hurt, and dead. No destination in mind, but the need to escape. Troy had fallen.

And now I was leaving.

IV. Nowhere

Are you surprised? Have I shocked you? Did you think you knew where the story was going? That I would go with Menelaus, that we'd be returning to Sparta, detailing the drama of those days, rebuilding our relationship, meeting with Odysseus again, learning the fate of Nest.

But instead, this. Turning away from what you know and taking you somewhere new. Not even letting you know where I'll be. I've titled this Nowhere, because that's where I was, it's where we all were, all those of us who fled Troy.

Back to that in-between time and place.

I'm sure there's consternation amongst some of you – cries that this is impossible. Such a swap could never happen, such an escape is unlikely, no one could attempt or survive such self-mutilation, the entire story is mad.

Madder than the son of a goddess being invulnerable everywhere except his heel? The world believes that easily enough.

That is what happened, as far as I remember it, and since I am not sitting in the palace at Sparta, I must assume at least some of that memory is correct. I know I've given you some hints, so this can't be a complete surprise. A taste of where I am. I'm sure you've found this frustrating; why hint and not just tell you? I'm getting to that. I haven't had much chance to shock people in my life, except with my face, and I think that choice, the choice to leave Troy like that, was the only time I really will in these pages. Please let me enjoy it.

So, what now?

Now I take you into the unknown. I daresay this will be the least interesting part for you; it does not involve war or heroes or much derring-do. But for me, it is the most important, it is when I took my own path which led me to where I sit now.

But there's still a way to go before that, and I need to chart that in-between time; between Troy and home, when I was nowhere. The devastation of the aftermath, the desolation of a displaced people. How we, the survivors of the sack of Troy, survived, and continued on. How I survived and became a new person. And, of course, answer the newest question you have; what did I look like? What do I look like now?

You know that is what you're wondering; all the drama and pain and details fade before it. What did that act of vandalism achieve? How far did the most beautiful woman fall, and by her own hand? I'll get to that, never fear.

Aftermath

I can't recall much of what happened after I was loaded onto that ship. My mind disconnected from my body, so even when I was awake, I wasn't there. What I recall most is the smell. The vomit and shit and pus of those around me. Of myself. And the decay. Those that died where they lay, and no one noticed. Or maybe they did, but didn't, or couldn't, care.

I also remember the sounds, but they were vague. The wailing and hacking and squelching and moaning. I couldn't hear it well though, it was all muffled. If I'd been conscious of my surroundings, that would have worried me, caused more fear, made me wonder what else I'd hurt other than my face. But I wasn't really there and was not able to think or notice it.

How long were we at sea? It could have been days or weeks. We could have been a single ship or thousands. I was insensible. But I was alive. I think, even in that dark and dank time, I understood that. Clung to it. Someone must have been seeing to me; giving me water and food, cleaning my wounds. The woman at the shore perhaps? I'll never know. Such acts were not spoken of later. Maybe because it was hard to think about that time, to think of how an extra drop of water for one person caused the death of another. No one wants that on their conscience. Or maybe we all wanted to forget, to agree it was unreal, it didn't really happen, it was nothing.

It was only when I was moved, jolted, when whoever it was tended my wounds that I truly came too. Searing flashes of hot pain dazzling me to wakefulness before I'd slump back into darkness. Pain will do that. But I can't recall how often that happened. All the pain of that time melds into one.

When I did eventually open my eyes with some sense of self, with some clarity that allowed my mind to work, when I was able to keep them open for more than a moment, I was puzzled by what I saw. Dirty white above me, blurred and spotted. In that moment I wondered if that's what the blind see, not darkness, but light.

It was my addled mind playing games with me. It was a sail, used as a makeshift cover. All the sails were being used like that. More useful to us as shelter than a way to move across the sea.

I learned later what had happened to us. After Troy fell, most of the ships in that harbour made it safely away; of course, they did, the Greeks had hidden their ships or ripped them apart for horse parts and were not using them as part of the attack. The ships of Troy sailed away and were able to make land on an island. Or at least most of them did; no one knew how many had fled, so it was hard to know how many had made it. The singers say that island was Delos, though it was more like a small spurt of land in the sea than a proper island. The important thing is that there was water, and food, and space.

Space is what we needed the most.

I say we. I suppose that's right. When I first arrived at Troy, they said I was now Trojan, I was given the moniker Helen of Troy, and yet, I was never really one of them. I was always separate. But after the fall, once I'd escaped, I was truly one of them. One of the few hundred who had escaped the city, whose entire world had been torn apart, who were injured, hurt, and heartbroken.

We were all recovering. Most had physical hurts to mend; I was not the only one burnt, so my injuries went unnoticed, but there were also broken limbs, open wounds, gouged eyes, bleeding inside bodies we couldn't see. And many did not survive. I think that might be the saddest thing, surviving the destruction, escaping to a type of safety, and then dying anyway.

More than that, everyone had hearts to mend.

I'm trying to think of how to describe this camp, this make-shift Troy. It was a sea of dirty whites and browns, all manner of fabric, but mostly ship sails with some ships dismantled to create lean-tos. It was a sharp contrast to the blue of the sea, yellow of the sand, the green of the sparse vegetation.

And then there were the people; bandaged, dirty, defeated.

Because when I think of that time, even as I know I was lost in my own world, as anyone who needs to heal must be, I cannot help but be pulled down by the utter desolation that enveloped that camp.

But how to make you understand? I'm not sure you ever can, unless you have lost your home, your everything, in such a way, and must sleep in a tent on a foreign shore. We were broken, and it wrapped itself around us like a cloak, making the most basic tasks, even breathing, a challenge. The camp was full of people but was so quiet; it was eerie to walk through it and hear so little of human life. The manual tasks that could not be avoided, as hard as they were, were done with vigour, because they stopped everyone from thinking, from feeling. But in the evening, it was impossible to ignore; talk was limited, any laughter was strained, life was stilled. Silence and sadness and shock reigned.

I know I am not doing it justice.

But how can I?

The aftermath of Troy might have been glorious for the Greeks, but for the remaining Trojans, it was devastation.

Beauty Means Nothing

And what of me?

I felt that devastation as well, but I would be lying if I said mine wasn't tinged with hope. Hope that I would be able to find a new path in the world, hope for my future. But immediately, I felt mostly pain.

There were so many injured, I was surrounded by pain, and mine didn't always seem that important. Tending to the sick and dying was what most of the able-bodied women did during that time. We were lucky that there were at least two healers; a doctor and a slave woman, but with so many they couldn't see to all of us.

The doctor, Iapyx, was an older man, stern and grey, though his face suggested he had laughed a lot once. He did see to me, more than once, while the slave woman, if we could think of her as such, would often be elsewhere. I thought little of it then, but if I consider it now, I realise that even amidst such times, they had created a hierarchy; I was surrounded by other finely dressed and bejewelled people. The doctor saw to the elite, and the slave saw to the commoners. There were fewer of the former, since the elite did not live by the smelly, busy, harbour. The harbour that saved so many lives. I wonder, out of the two groups, how many survived?

It was Iapyx who came up to talk to me once I regained my senses.

He crouched beside me, offering me water. Then he raised my head and looked into my eyes. I remember thinking he looked lopsided.

"I think the madness has passed. For now." I can still hear that clearly. I wonder what I had been babbling about. It has become a saying of mine. One that causes the servants to roll their eyes at me.

He sat me up and waited to see how I'd do. It was a little disorientating, after spending so much time (but how much time?) lying flat. It disturbed the bedsores that had developed and caused my muscles to scream in protest, my vision to swim, and my head to ache and burn as I'd never felt before. It was almost worse than childbirth.

"You can understand me?" the healer asked. I tried to speak but could only croak, so I nodded but that caused more pain, like my brain was sloshing around my skull.

He took my hand. "Squeeze once for yes, twice for no, do not squeeze if you do not know or understand the question. Do you understand?"

I squeezed his hand.

He started asked me questions. Did I know my name? Was I Trojan? Was I a lady of means? Did my head hurt? Did my arm hurt? And so on. I had to lie, I knew I did, but at least not too much, after all, hadn't everyone in the palace told me I was now Trojan, wasn't I a princess, didn't I have burns across my face, bruises everywhere? As for my name, there was only one I could use – Lena. It was me, it was mine, though so few people had ever called me by it. If it gave Iapyx pause, this dark lady having a name so like ones whispered around the palace, murmured as part of the gossip of the city, he didn't show it. I wonder now how many of the displaced of Troy found new names, new identities, on that island, created a new past to help them forge a new future. I was surely not alone.

Eventually he asked me if I wanted to know what had happened since we left Troy. I squeezed twice. I didn't want to know then; I knew I'd find out eventually, and at that moment, I knew I couldn't contain the facts, the gossip, any more pain. I could see the confusion on his face. He repeated the question, and I squeezed twice again.

He seemed stunned. Then asked if I wanted to know about my condition. To this I squeezed yes.

This was the first step in finding out what I'd done to myself.

He told me I had severe burns along my face and head. Which I already knew. He told me someone had tried to clean the wound and had bandaged it with honey. My mystery woman, I assumed; she earned those bracelets. When I'd been brought onto the island and set in his care, he'd replaced the bandage. He'd had to cut the rest of my hair as it had been matted with blood and soot and who knew what else.

He said that the burns were extensive. That he wasn't sure what the outcome would be. But that I would certainly look different. He was sure I'd lost the use of my eye, though it still seemed to be in place. He guessed that ear, deformed as it would be, would be useless too. He told me my lips on that side were gone, which might lead to dribbling and make it difficult to speak. That I'd apparently escaped infection was a blessing. That I had survived so far was a good sign. But that was likely as far as any luck would take me.

I listened carefully. I didn't respond in any way. I just let him list the ways I had changed myself. Finally, he asked me if I understood. I squeezed his hand, set my head back, and went back to sleep.

It stayed like that for a while. I'd doze in and out. A young woman would feed me whatever pulped mush she had and drip water into my mouth. And sometimes the healer would come by.

Healing takes time. No matter what it's from, and mine took a long time. I had damaged myself in a way no one should be damaged. My skin scabbed over and healed with scars, but it wasn't until long after I left that island that I had again what might be called a face. And even then, very few would ever see it.

Of course, at some point the bandages had to come off and stay off.

I had no surface to see myself, and Iapyx advised against it. His face was well schooled, he showed no emotion as he peeled away whatever he was using as a cover; I wondered if he'd tended to the soldiers of Troy, was used to seeing disturbing and disfiguring wounds. The young woman who assisted him still had things to learn. Her look of horror told me all I needed to know.

When I ran my hand over the tender skin that now was my face, I could feel areas of strange slickness and softness, alongside patches of rough. I could tell that my ear was now more of a nub. My head had been shaved, but I could feel the clear line between what had been caught in the fire and what hadn't, on one side was soft down, and on the other any hair that grew was coarse and bristly. I was told my eyelid sagged, though the doctor was right, I'd lost my sight in that eye, so I suppose it didn't matter. And my lips were not exactly gone, but twisted and limp, constantly open on that side of my face. Almost everything hurt, especially when I touched it, but what scared me more were the parts that didn't hurt, where I didn't feel a thing.

As much as I appreciated Iapyx's advice, I knew I needed to see myself. My explorations only told me so much, I needed to see what I looked like. It was the young woman who finally agreed to help me; she brought me a small mirror, poor quality and burnished. Who knows where she found it. I knew it would distort me further, but it was better than nothing.

The most shocking thing to me was the colour; it was pink and red. Bright, bold, and contrasting with the rest of my face. Some spaces were dirty with scabs. Once adjusted, I could see my eye was a milky white and my lips were gaping, my mouth twisting to compensate, still dribbling. My nose was mostly intact but seemed to cave in on one side.

I was like Janus, the two-faced god, but the rawness of the left side of my face also impacted the right. It seemed to make that hideous as well; the green cat eye now looked malevolent, the high cheekbone a hideous stretch of skin, my full lips inflated lumps that should be limp. And my hair, shorn roughly to my scalp but starting to grow again, became a sick crown distorting my features.

How did I feel when the result was revealed to me? Scared. Sick. Shocked. I think I vomited. I had spent so long with one face, and now I had a new one. My aim had been to make myself unrecognisable, to destroy my own beauty, and I had succeeded. I doubt either Menelaus or Paris would recognise me now.

Did I regret doing it? Perhaps, in that moment, as the reality sank in as it had never done before. I really was no longer Helena of Troy. No one would look at me with lust or desire or an eye to power. In fact, most people wouldn't look at me at all.

Many nobles in such a position would have a mask made and hide inside their walls. Now, as I go about my life, I have adopted veils, it makes it easier to get things done, and doubles to keep the heat and flies at bay. But back then, being stranded on a camp on an island far from anyone, not wanting anyone to find us, it removed that option, and so my face was on display for everyone to see. Not that I was alone; there were many of us who had disfigurements; limbs had been lost, skin had been burnt, and we all feared disease would come for us. Compared to others, I was practically healthy, still able-bodied, my brain no more addled than it was before. Others were not so lucky, and we all knew Iapyx was making decisions, taking life into his own hands. The funeral pyres were lit on the other side of the island, away from the camp, but with so many dead there was a fear of discovery. I never asked what they did with the other bodies. No one asked.

As I was able bodied, once Iapyx was happy, I was expected to get involved in the camp, to contribute to keeping us all alive. I suspect had I been back in Troy or Sparta, I would not have been allowed to work so soon, but what were we to do? I don't know how long we'd been there when I was sent to that group of women who took charge of the tasks women did. There was a group of men making decisions, but by the time I was ready, there was a rhythm to the camp, and an order to be followed.

I was slowly introduced to tasks around the camp, and no one questioned that I knew so little of cooking, washing, cleaning, anything really, except sewing and plants. At first, I could only do the most basic tasks anyway, I was too tired and ill to do more.

It was a shock. The work of living. Of having to fight and scrape and scrounge for survival. And of having to do so surrounded by so many others trying to do the same.

You're probably laughing at me right now. The spoiled princess, who doesn't know what a hard day's work is like, who has always had servants and slaves to cater to her every whim! And in many ways, it was true; I've already said that now, as an old lady, I see that even a gilded cage is still gilded, and so much better than one of cold, dank earth. Even as I strained against my life, it was, in so many ways, easier than so many others.

That is something I learned on that island with the survivors of Troy. At first, I was still healing, I couldn't physically do much, and then I had to learn how to do some of the tasks even children thought were simple, such as collecting kindling. I had no idea how tiresome that could be, how heavy even light sticks could feel in the arms of someone who has already worked a day and sleeps on the ground. I was typically hungry, as was everyone, but it was a feeling I'd never known before. The curves that had first enticed then disgusted Paris truly disappeared now, and the hollowness that came into my face distorted my features further. I could feel my bones poking out of my skin when I lay on the light sacking I used as a bed, and the ground poked back, harder.

This is the point where I need to discuss the virtues I learned here. The resilience of people, the satisfaction of a hard day's work, the camaraderie of the shared experience. I suppose some of that is true to an extent. And without that time, without learning how to work, how to survive, I most certainly would not have been able to later. But honestly, even while I see that it helped, no one should have to live like that. And I was glad when I didn't have to anymore.

As for the people, they were resilient, as survivors often are. But I'd be lying if I said I built up a bond with them. Surviving together is a strong bond, don't get me wrong, but I feared being recognised, and everyone was healing. That devastation made bonding hard.

I suppose it was the court of Sparta all over again. Knowing I should try, that I should work to get to know the people around me, to form attachments. In my defence, I was around people as I hadn't been for a long time; in Sparta, in Troy, I had more often been kept away from people, and only really interacted when I was being paraded to showcase the power, the prestige, of that place.

I was also not the only one who resisted, or who stayed close to themselves. There were those who were forging a new identity, like me, and those who did not know how to talk. We did not know who we were living with, whom to trust. Just as we had to burn bodies succumbing to wounds from the battle and the harshness of survival, so to we had to burn those who were found after a scream was heard in the night – bodies stripped of valuables, fresh blood staining their clothes. No one spoke about it, and eventually it died down. We all just kept on working, interacting as we needed to, surviving.

I suppose it was this that made me aware of the lack of looking. I suppose, I'd become used to it. People were always looking at me. Or at least, those who were allowed around me. Servants and slaves, princes and generals, even women, those that I was allowed around, would stop in their tracks to stare, to gaze at me. Whether because I was beautiful, or because I was strange, or because people had been told I was both of those things, is irrelevant. I was used to being looked at. In many ways, I hadn't realised how used to it I was until I was disfigured and working on that island. How much that looking had formed the world around me. Or how much I accepted that I was a person to be looked at.

And now, I had to get used to not being looked at. Eyes would glaze over me. People would physically turn away. Instructions would be given to my shoulder, questions asked of my chest and stomach, comments made to my feet. It was like they thought that by looking at me, they might to become disfigured.

How did this feel? How after a lifetime of being looked at, praised, denigrated, did it feel to be ignored? I'm not sure. Everything was so different then, at least for me, that in some ways, it felt natural. I was Lena, of course people would not look at me. I think I also felt relief, if people weren't looking, then it was less likely that anyone would recognise me.

Anyway, was it that much different from being beautiful? It's been more than thirty years now, and I'd say yes. To be looked at with envy and wonder and lust, rather than pity and disgust; its different. Both may be hard, but the first is much preferred. Simply, it makes life easier. Though on that island, life was hard for everyone. It was easier for the men though; there were men more scarred than me, but they seemed more easily accepted. I guess they were expected to be scarred.

I'm used to it now, and now I'm so old it's difficult to tell my scars from my wrinkles. But it never goes away.

I cannot ask for much sympathy; I did it to myself, and in doing so I bought myself a new life. But still.

It was at that camp I also discovered that just because I was no longer considered beautiful, it didn't mean I was free of attention, or safe from the desires that had dictated so much of my life. I might not have been looked at with lust anymore, but that didn't mean I had stopped being a woman, and that meant I was still available to be used.

I described the camp as covered in desolation, and that was true, but desolation, much like terror, cannot be sustained. And even in desolation, men will still be men.

I can't imagine I was the only woman who had to fend off an attack in the camp. But I was still surprised. It was once I had started working with the other women, cleaning what food we could find, learning how to skin the meat the few hunters would bring us, clean the fish gathered from the sea. I was surprised that it was a young man, lean, strong, good-looking. Someone who could have had many willing women – there were plenty of those in the camp.

But I suppose he had decided he wanted me. Unwillingly. It was dark, I had gone to relieve myself, and he swaggered up, grabbing me from behind. Hissing in my ear so a string a saliva ran down my neck. Perhaps he thought I'd be so surprised, so grateful for this attention, I'd be silent, for he didn't cover my mouth or put his hand around my throat. Or maybe he didn't want to touch my face; to feel the slick skin under his hands. So instead of going quietly, as I have so many times before, I screamed. I screamed and wiggled as I hadn't when Paris had come upon me or Deiphobus had lunged. That had happened to Helena, but this happened to Lena, and Lena was angrier and stronger and uglier. Lena screamed.

This brought guards and others, and the man ran off, leaving me alone and shaking. I thought I'd see him, lurking around sometimes, and I made sure to avoid him, and to be alone as little as possible. Then one day he turned up drowned in the sea. It wasn't me who did it, but there were plenty of candidates, people who did not like this man. No one worried about it or tried to discover the murderer. We had too much else to do.

He wasn't alone in his attentions, but he was the only one who attacked. I'd get snide remarks, feel hands on my backside and thighs, see them looking openly at my breasts. But they wouldn't look at my face. And I had no royal rank to protect me.

That's when I realised something most of you probably already know. I had aways thought of my beauty in terms of me, but now I understood than when it came to men, beauty means little. It's not about your beauty to those men. It's about their power.

New Troy

There's so much about that time I find hard to recognise now; the years and seasons slide together into one. I do know that we were on that island from the summer, and it was getting colder when I left, though once winter came, we couldn't sail anywhere, so we were there for more than a year, maybe longer. That's plenty of time for the wheat to separate from the chaff, because while some fall apart after a tragedy, some rise to the occasion.

How long was it before people began muttering? Before conversation at the fire side turned to the horizon? Before someone proposed a new plan?

Here we were, the remnants of a great city, living like paupers, cast-aways, and no one had come to look for us. Thankfully, the Greeks appeared happy with what they had achieved, there were no searches or hunts from our enemies, but equally, there were no envoys or invitations from friends. After all, the Aegean isn't that big. We were on this island to heal, to gather our wits. But eventually, everyone knew we'd have to move on.

There's always someone with an idea, and that's all well and good, but the key is having the power to persuade others along with you. Paris was able to do that through his charm, blinding people to how terrible his ideas could be. Odysseus used his quick wit and quicker mind to see the best path to persuade whoever he was talking to. Agamemnon used brute force. Whereas for Cassandra, as clever as she was, her sex stopped anyone from taking note of her at all.

The leader, rising to the surface in that camp, had charisma, and a powerful, potent, dream.

Aeneas' smile was bright, brilliant, and lit up his whole face even when it didn't reach his eyes. He had the habit of touching everyone he met, gripping their hand, squeezing their shoulder, hugging them close. Something that everyone on that touch-starved island craved and valued. And his dream was simple; a new Troy, out west, away from the Greeks we'd fought, the Greeks we'd lost to. There were colonies and trade, and land, lots of it. And who would lead, who would be the new king of this new Troy? He would, of course. It was, after all, his plan.

I suppose it was inevitable. A leader was needed, a plan was required, a dream was wanted. How else could a people so broken be stitched back together? Is this how kings are made?

As time passed, his plan grew, as did his faith in himself. This young man, who had only gained access to the inner chamber of Priam's palace and confidences because other, better, men had died on the battlefield, started to present himself not only as a future king, but as a descendant of the gods themselves. Rivalling Achilles, and, of course, Helen of Troy; the children of gods, who set history on its path.

I find it interesting that he chose Aphrodite as his erstwhile divine mother. A patron of Troy, but also part of its downfall. Perhaps he felt the people had enough of war and cleverness and prophecy. They needed something else to bind them together. He did look the part of Cupid, handsome and strong, golden and young, and he followed the fashion of Paris, beard scruff barely covering his chin.

Aeneas would stand on a broken boulder and tell anyone who listened his plan. His vision, which was now more than an idea, but a real prophecy sent by the gods, with his mother watching over them. People did gather, they did listen, and I watched as I saw the dream grow.

Once he invoked the gods, I made sure to avoid him, keep myself away. I'd never seen him at the palace, and it seemed unlikely he'd recognise me even if I had. But still, I didn't want any suspicions to fall on me. I knew that he would need a royal bride, sooner or later, and had no desire for that to be me. At that point I was certain I would never attain husband number 3.

I remember sitting with a circle of women whilst we prepared food – chopped and skinned and seasoned and preserved – talking about nothing of consequence, telling stories. This is where I first heard the stories of Helen of Troy, told with venom and occasionally with sympathy. We were an odd bunch, those considered too weak or noble to really get our hands dirty. This meant we were a mixture of the old and disfigured, the rich and poor, the free and enslaved – though there were few who could rarely be considered slaves on that island. Still, I enjoyed listening to them. I rarely contributed more than a few words, some knowledge on plants or stitches. Talk often turned to Aeneas and his plans, and as they grew, so did the conversation.

Or The Talk. That's how everyone referred to it. The Talk.

In our circle, all the different views and opinions seemed to exist. The younger ones, the poorer ones, were enamoured of Aenaes' plan. The older, wealthier, wanted to return to Troy, to be laid to rest in the tombs of their ancestors. Some thought we should stay on this island; the spot was nice enough, why go sailing across the seas when we could build a new city here? And there were others who wanted to go to one of the established cities, restart there, away from everything. We could even send messengers, envoys, wait for responses, be formal about it all.

I fell into the last group. I spent the winter thinking a lot and I knew I didn't want to stay with these people, as nice as they were. I wanted to be away from all of this. Away from Trojans and Greeks, and their stories and wars.

It was Melita, the same young woman who had nursed me in the sick tent, who spoke most ardently about Aeneas' plan. It seems she was more devout than any of us.

"He has been directed by the gods" I remember her saying. "They have not abandoned us. We are the survivors, they have plans for us. A bigger, better, stronger empire than Troy ever was. We just need to find it."

Melita didn't look Trojan in the same way I didn't look Greek. A slave or a servant seemed most likely; she looked eastern, her hair was straight and black, her skin pale.

Someone asked her how. How will they find a city that doesn't yet exist? As with all true-believers, Melita knew we just had to trust in the gods, they would show us the way.

Hearing this was the first time I'd laughed in a long time, though it sounded more like a strange gurgle, and my lips were not able to produce a clear smile anymore. If I tried to smile, I could feel the muscles contorting and the skin stretching in an unnatural way.

"You find that funny" she asked.

It was unusual for me to speak, and in my recollection, everyone's attention is turned to me. Waiting to hear my every word. Looking in my direction, but not actually looking at me.

But I might be misremembering.

"There are so many men who think the gods have great things in store for them. Often, those paths lead to death. We are the result of just that. I'm not sure I can see much difference between great things and terrible ones."

I could feel the mutterings around me. I can't imagine there weren't people in that group who didn't think the same; that this talk of gods and greatness was what had led us all here, had destroyed Troy in the first place. It stank of hubris.

The look Melita gave me though, turned me cold, and I wondered what this girl had seen, what her life had been. Even as I judged her to be a servant, someone from far away, I forgot what that might mean. "Perhaps, but men, and women, can dream of great things for themselves. And can set out to achieve them."

“Those things can still be terrible” I said sharply, I disliked where this was going. I disliked that I was being contradicted, that this girl couldn’t see how the promise of divine favour could deliver horror and death. And, if I’m being honest, I disliked being spoken to on equal terms. I was still adjusting to my new life, and whilst I was careful to be respectful, to listen, to act along with the others, that sense of pride, of specialness, of superiority, at least to those beneath me, still lingered. I wasn’t used to this type of conversation with someone I thought of as lower than me, it had so rarely happened. I’ve adjusted since, or at least, I hope I have.

“Only for those who lose” her reply came just as quick.

“Troy has lost” I was blunt, unemotional. It was a fact.

She nodded. “But I’m not Trojan, I never was. None of us are anymore. Perhaps I, we, have a home in a new city.”

With that she stood, collected her basket of work, and walked away. She never seemed to be at work with our group after that. At least, I can’t remember her. I suppose I offended her. I would see her sometimes, sitting at the feet of Aeneas, with the gaggle of other women who seemed to trail behind him, but that was always from afar and I never really saw her up close again. When I think of her now, I think of her walking away; straight-backed, proud. And I feel ashamed, even if what I’d said was true.

Eventually, we had to decide; not as a group, but each of us. What were we to do?

I think that’s when Troy, the idea of Troy, really ended. When its survivors split and went their separate ways. After that, there weren’t any Trojans, despite what Aeneas might have said or might have told those he met on his journey.

We became Athenians, Thebans, Phoenicians. A scattered people, searching for a new home, with no reason or desire to remember the past.

Troy was dead.

Aeneas left first. The young, the full-bodied, the fool-hardy went with him, hoping for excitement, adventure, to be the new heroes of a new city. With him went most of the ships and provisions; no one argued with this, those of us left were the old, infirm, and dreamless, how could we argue.

I've heard vague stories of Aeneas since; stories filtered through that he was King of Carthage or killed their Queen, but nothing more. Either he founded his city, his new Troy, far away from civilization, or he's dead. Or he needs to create a better story.

That left to rest of us to decide what to do. Some people, some groups, left of their own accord, sometimes out in the open, waving goodbye in the sunlight. But sometimes slipping away in the night, stealing what others had, leaving no message or idea of their destination. There wasn't much we could do except make sure we kept all out belongings, all our valuables, close. This included the food, though when the guard slips off as well, what can you do?

Soon bigger groups began to leave, like Aeneas; one ship did leave to return to Troy, mostly full of older people, going back to see what could be reclaimed from the ashes, to be buried at home. Another left to go to one of the Greek cities, perhaps Corinth, to see if relief might be felt amongst the Greeks, to see if they could find their loved ones.

Neither of these appealed to me. But as our numbers dwindled, I could feel a sort of low panic take hold of me. I needed to go somewhere, and I would need help getting there.

I did, you might be surprised to know, still have my jewels and gold, or some of them. When I woke up in that make-shift doctor's tent, my bracelets and armlets were gone, as were my necklaces, but my rings were still on my fingers and toes – bruised from someone trying to remove them. I always did swell easily; I'm almost surprised I didn't lose some appendages. Some of the pieces sewn in the hem of my dress were intact, some lost as the fabric had ripped, and a small purse sewn inside my dress remained as well. Perhaps most shockingly of all, my swan brooch still sat on my chest; it was small and burnished, so perhaps no one saw it, or thought it valuable. I cannot tell you how happy I was to discover it when I woke. A small piece of me, all the versions of me.

The amount I had was not as much as I was once bedecked with, but these had helped me once before, when I stood before Priam. I knew that my life, was linked to them. I was ready to use them again.

In the end, they weren't needed. At least not then. One group decided they would travel to Egypt; there were Greek and Trojan settlements there, and it was far enough away from Agamemnon and the Greek kings to feel safe. Egypt was a name heard in whispers; they were mysterious, rich, and worshipped animals. Most importantly, they had not been involved in the war, nor were they among the friends Troy had once thought it had. For me, it sparked my interest; it was exotic and exciting. But more than that, I remembered Lena, the new Helena of Troy, had told me she was from beyond Egypt. I wondered if I could find something of me there, or something for the new me.

It was the third time I was to set sail upon the sea; this time more-or-less whole and hearty and excited about the future. I loved every moment, with the sun, the horizon, the smell, and the spray. I think I even saw some dolphins, it felt like a good omen. If I'd known I'd never travel on it again, I probably would have enjoyed it more. I had no idea I was heading towards home; towards a life I wouldn't want to risk leaving.

In all our stories, when the hero is travelling by sea, there is a storm. A huge storm that causes the ship to be dragged off course, and our hero must brave some horror before returning to their journey. I, if I can call myself a hero, was no different.

Crossing the sea is safer outside of winter, but not without peril. A storm still managed to come upon us, and we were not manned by the best sailors; they had gone with Aeneas. We were tossed around like a toy, pushed off course, and by the time the storm broke, it had taken a good portion of the ship with it. We still made it to Egypt, but not where we planned or as regally as we'd planned. We had no choice but to limp into the nearest harbour, a natural harbour with a small fishing village on the tip of the country. Nothing much but some huts and a tiny temple.

Still, more than we'd come from I suppose. The villagers, though wary and speaking in a strange manner, were friendly enough. They provided some food and water, then sent us to set up camp a little way from the village. Far enough to feel safe, close enough that they could keep an eye on us. It seems unlikely we were the first ship to come ashore at Rhakotis in need.

But we were here, and we couldn't help but ask: what would we do now? Our plans had been thwarted, we had changed an island beach for a mainland beach, we were once again stranded, many had lost what little belongings they had to the sea, and we were not in the civilization we'd envisaged. This was no Greek city, with a familiar language and possible friends. Still though, we were in Egypt, and that was something.

And we were tired. I remember feeling so tired. I'm not sure any of us could have travelled further then if we'd wanted to. It might sound strange, we'd spent more than a year healing, and surely, we'd felt strong enough to travel. All these things are true. But living through tempest after tempest, it drains you. In many ways, our situation hadn't changed – here was another beach, another foreign land – but also, here were people to talk to, to learn from, a settlement to join rather than build. And our ship wouldn't be taking to the water again for a long time; once we could see it, I was amazed it had brought us to shore at all.

I think we decided without talking. This was it. At least for now.

So, I, or we, those from the ship, joined this tiny community, slipped into the rhythm of life at Rhakotis. We kept our own gods, and while we learnt to speak to them, we spoke Greek to each other. Eventually, an Egyptian man of the village, and a Trojan woman, married. We build small huts for our own homes. I did not have a room to myself, but I shared a sleeping space with four other women (three after the marriage). Some of the men went out fishing. Some of the women began to sew and keep livestock and grow a small garden.

As I think on it, I learned so much at that village. In a different way to before. There was stability here as there never was on that island, the joy of choice. It was still hard, still a fight for survival, but less so; there were people, and resources, and hope. As the fear and disappointment of the storm passed, it was possible to see how different and safe Rhakotis was from where I'd been before. I wouldn't stay there, but if I hadn't been there, if we hadn't come ashore there, I'm not sure I would have survived as I have.

It was peaceful. We were healing. We worked together. We tried to make a life.

No one spoke of Troy. Those lives were over.

For me, it was a haven, and the rhythm of village life suited me far better than the rigors of a refugee camp. I was able to walk alone, which felt like the most wonderful gift. I would steal away early in the morning, as the fishermen began to set out their boats, or in the evening as the cooking fires wafted the smell of roasted fish over the village, and I would stroll along the beach. I would gaze out at the sea, and I would let it all wash over me. In some ways, I think that was the greatest, the most important, thing I did at Rhakotis – let the sea heal me, mind and spirit.

I kept my distance from the other Trojans, and Egyptians though with them it was easier as we could not speak. Even as I shared a hut with those women, I stayed contained – speaking only when spoken to, getting on with chores, slipping away to be along when I could. I'm sure they noticed, though again, I wasn't the only one. More than once, I'd return to our hut to a sudden silence, a sign they'd been speaking about me before I entered.

So why didn't I try to make friends here? Why be Helena the aloof, the isolated? Why not become Lena the talker, the friend-maker? As I think back on it, I know that I was still healing and becoming used to this new world, as well as the new me. Technically, that should be reason enough. But it's not. Even then, I knew I would not be staying with these people forever, though I stayed longer than I should. I knew I would want, need, to leave, and that would be so much easier if I wasn't enmeshed with them.

This is why I did the one thing I am slightly ashamed of.

Once I knew I would stay for at least a little while, in the middle of that night, I stole away from everyone and found a scraggly tree with some odd boulders nearby. I took my stash of gold and gems, and I buried it there. I didn't want to share. I didn't want to use it to barter for supplies. I wanted to keep it hidden and safe for me to use, as I knew I would. Sharing a space, being more open, would make that difficult, so I hid it all.

How selfish of me, I know. I could have shared it, could have used it to purchase supplies, build homes, clothe, and feed us, get us to one of those cities. But even when I'd scarred my face, I'd still been vulnerable to men; I'd already been driven from two homes. I wanted insurance. I wanted to feel safe. I wanted to be prepared for the inevitable.

I very occasionally went and added to it if it came across anything I thought worthwhile. I even occasionally hid a waxed bag with food in case I needed to leave quickly. Though I never did, and typically ate what I had hidden when walking along the beach. It was a beautiful beach, and the sea was strong and choppy, I walked it as often as I could. I loved being outdoors, and as much as I worked with everyone, I enjoyed being alone more. I think they preferred that as well; then they didn't have to look at my face.

That's how we all lived; the rhythm of life reasserting itself. That might be how some are still living up in Rhakotis. I wouldn't know. I a few years there, 2 I think, maybe more, maybe less. Then I left.

Odysseus Again

The only story more popular than Troy is that of Odysseus. It seems to be retold wherever you go, and always leads to cheers. Perhaps because it's more of an adventure, has a happier ending. In some ways that's become more famous that the war itself. I know that what the poets write about is only half the story, and the reason I know, is because I met him again, on the shores of Egypt.

We'd been at Rhakotis a long time, or so I think; again, time plays its tricks on me, and my memory plays them even more. Troy's fall was still fresh but becoming old as the years started to stretch out. My face was well healed, or as healed as it would ever be by then. We were all living this quiet life; sometimes easy when the weather was pleasant, and the fish were plentiful, harder when the sea battered the shore, and the fish were elsewhere. But safe and hopeful.

It was all new to me, of course. This quiet, this way of living life as the world around you turns. I daresay, it's what was needed after 9 years of war.

And then, on the horizon, another ship came into view.

I was the one that found the ship of course. I was walking along the beach at low tide, and I saw it ahead. I recognised it for one of the Greek ships immediately. How could I not?

I was startled, and one of the greatest fears I have ever known swept over me. I'd been scared before, for myself or others. I've lived through war, rape, abduction, escape. But seeing that ship caused a fear so strong I vomited. I just kept thinking 'they've found me. They've found me. They've found me'.

But they hadn't, because they weren't looking for me.

At the sight of it, I almost ran away then and there. I would have left my bag of treasure and run straight into the wild, away from the village. But luckily for me, someone else had seen them to, so by the time the ship was ready to come in, I could hide behind everyone else.

A delegation was sent out to find out what was happening. There was something wrong with the ship, so they stayed for a few weeks whilst they fixed it, and soon the Greek sailors were sitting around our fires, sharing stories and news and gossip with the Trojans. As though a few years before they weren't trying to kill each other. I both tried, and tried not, to hear if there was any gossip about Helena of Troy, but either they didn't know any or didn't care much about that subject. I wasn't sure if I was relieved or annoyed.

My fear seemed to have been misplaced, my plan appeared to have worked. None of them looked at me. Like everyone else, their eyes slide over my face, away from me. They were sailors, they'd been at sea for long months, they didn't want to see a battle scarred and ugly woman. There were plenty of other options around them.

But Odysseus was smart. He was observant. He had a good memory. He was the one I tried to avoid the most. But it was a small village, and no one else wanted to avoid the great hero of Troy.

It was evening, and I was watching the last of the sun set on the beach, at one of my favourite spots. Away from everyone.

He came and sat next to me.

We sat in silence for a while. Both of us staring out across the water.

So much of my life is half-remembered, has merged through time and circumstance so it's hard to know exactly what happened and in what order. But this I remember clearly, as though it happened only moments ago. And when I think of it, my heart still aches.

"How did you know?"

He sighed. "You look like you".

I turned to him then. He was sitting on the side of my scar; the creased and layered flesh always pink, the strange fuzz that grew instead of hair, my permanently curled lip, nub for an ear, and milky eye.

"I do not." A simple fact.

He smiled and turned to face me too. He looked older. His face was lined and weather-beaten, with sores on his lips, his hair was grey like stone and his beard was long and unkempt. But his eyes were the same.

"Yes, you do. You look like Helen. You move like Helen. You sound like Helen. Far more so than the woman Menelaus brought out of that damned city".

"Did he tell you?"

"He didn't have to. I saw it immediately. I thought you were probably dead though. Poison was my guess."

"The cowards way?"

He chuckled. "The quiet way."

"And?" I needed to know.

"And what?"

"What did you do? About the other Helen"

"There is no other Helen" he said clearly. "She is Helen. Queen of Sparta, wife of Menelaus. Mother of his children. His recent children." He corrected.

I was caught by that. I'm not sure why. She was young and fresh and beautiful. Of course, they'd have children. Of course.

"And she's a good queen." Odysseus continued

"Better than me?" I could feel a smile tugging on my lips at that, at the good side at least.

"No. You didn't do or say anything. You were the perfect queen." Odysseus' response startled me.

"I think you'll find few would agree with you." I could hear the bitterness in my voice, and I was surprised by it. Until that moment, I hadn't realised I'd been holding on to it; the anger and bitterness at what had happened to me.

"They don't know what happened. What we did. What we didn't do." Odysseus looked ashamed in that moment.

"You mean what you did."

He winced. "What I did." He agreed.

"Was it worth it?" I asked.

"It's always worth it. It must be."

I nodded. "But was it worth it?"

He shook his head gently and looked away. I thought I saw tears in his eyes. And I felt something loosen in me.

"Was I worth it?" I asked.

"It was never about you, you know" He was still facing away.

"And yet."

He turned back and opened his mouth to say something. But closed it. For a moment I thought he was going to say sorry. Say sorry for using me as a game piece. As I sat there looking at him, looking at this great man who was still just a man, I felt that bit of anger slip away. I didn't need him to apologise. He probably wouldn't. I just needed the acknowledgement, and I needed to let him, let them all, go.

I swallowed. He was right after all; it had never been about me.

"And now? Why haven't you gone home?"

"Why didn't you?" He was defensive again.

"Because I didn't want to. I wanted…to be free".

"And are you?" He asked.

I paused before answering. Was I free? What was I doing here? I was able to come and go, I was learning and healing, but was this the freedom I wanted. I realised that in many ways, I was ghost, just as much a lost prop as I'd been before. It hit me then that I was still surviving. And surviving is important. Surviving is vital. But at some point, you need to move on to living, because surviving is not enough, and it's not worth it. Just as the anger, the bitterness had lifted from me, so something else clicked into place, and my mind strayed to that hidden bag of treasure.

"Not yet. But I will be soon," I said.

He nodded. He understood, I think. I thought back to that young man I'd seen all those years ago. The brash, arrogant, manipulative young man who had spoken so cruelly about me to his friend, who had used my wedding to weave his own web of plans. This man sitting next to me was different. He had been humbled. Not too much, he was still and always will be swift Odysseus. But I think he knew so much more now.

"You don't want to go home" I said, it was a statement not a question.

He looked away again. He seemed to have lost the ability to look at me when telling the truth. Perhaps it was my face, but I thought not in this case. Maybe it was because he'd become so used to lying "I'm not sure I can. I can't go home and what? Sit on a throne? Rule an island?"

"Be with your wife and child?" I responded.

"And tell them about the glories of the siege of Troy? Of the rats and shit and mud and blood. And how the fall of that city let out ten years of rage. You saw it?"

"I saw some of it". I conceded.

"Would you want to tell your children about that?"

"And will sailing forever help? Will staying with different women help?"

He looked sheepish then. "You've heard about that?"

"Your men speak of little else. They're surprised you haven't found another lover here".

"Maybe I have" and he reached out to stroke my cheek. My scarred cheek.

I didn't smack him away or startle. Instead, I gently laid my hand over his and moved it to his knee as I shook my head.

He smiled again, sadly. "Is it me?"

"It's everyone" I said. And he nodded.

"You've changed" he said simply, "I don't mean your face. I mean you."

"I'm older" I said, a chuckle in my voice.

"Yes, but more than that. When I first met you, you were this quiet, demur thing, and now…you're sitting on a beach in the dark talking to a known rogue."

He was right. I'd never really spoken to any man like this. Openly, frankly, about what really mattered. It felt like a sign I was ready.

"I suppose that makes both of us then." And he nodded in agreement.

The sun had set by this point. The breeze was picking up and there was a chill in the air. I stood to leave.

"I hope you find your freedom" he said. He stayed seated.

“I hope you find yours too” I said, watching him stare into the darkness. I’m not sure how long he stayed there. I didn’t look back.

We never got another chance to talk; they left the next day. I stood with the crowd, and I thought I saw him looking for me. He waved slightly, and I nodded. Odysseus returned home eventually, I doubt it took 10 years, but I’m sure it wasn’t after our conversation. Still, I hope when he got there, he did find what he needed, just as I have.

As the ship sailed away, I walked to my buried treasure. I pulled out my torn and bloodied dress which held the gold and jewels with which I’d fled Troy. I remember looking at it all carefully, counting it, thinking what it could get me. I placed them into the woven bag I had taken to keeping with me and went back to the village, considering how I would leave.

Thinking about what I wanted, what I needed, to be truly free.

V. Egypt

I'm coming to the end of my story. You must have worked out that this is the final section, the place I 'end up'. With a home in Egypt, a partner, a life far away from kings and princesses and gods. That's where all those teases and tastes were leading you.

When I go to the market, travel along the river, or head to one of the large towns, I hear the different stories being told, the songs being sang, about the War at Troy, the Fall of Ilium. It's a good story, or rather, they're good stories because there's more than one. It doesn't matter if you're Greek, Trojan, Egyptian, Kushite; everyone understands war and glory, love and tragedy, humility and hubris, gods and men. And this story has it all. This is how, why, I know about the tales they tell about me, the story seems to be everywhere. And the others, the other stories linked to Troy, mostly tragic, like Nest, Agamemnon, Odysseus. There are many stories, some contradict themselves, and others have hints of the truth; there's one that tells that Helen was never really 'of Troy' at all, but instead was whisked away and hidden in Egypt throughout the war. Sometimes, stories hit close to the truth by accident.

My story has been one of so many events, intrigues, great men, travels, and now we fall away from that. I find myself most reluctant to tell this part. Why is that? I've shown you the darkest parts of me; my vanity, my ignorance, my abuse. But here, at the final hurdle, the happiest part, I find it hard to tell you.

I think I know why, and you might be able to guess it to. It's because its close. Close to my heart, less fractured by memory, with witnesses sitting around me. Almost as if, by putting it down on papyrus, I'll lose it all.

So, forgive me if you feel this is leaving out important points, details, making everything seem easy. Forgive me if you feel this part is untethered, that I wonder and wander too much. If you find that you, and I, feel slightly loose. My life up to this point is told and retold, shaped, and changed by everyone from kings to paupers. Even though I'm telling you it here, I find I'd still like to keep some of it for myself.

The Nile

In all my life, I have never seen anything as beautiful as the Nile.

The endless stretch of the sea had drawn me to it. The calm, bright beaches had soothed me. The rhythm of my loom had comforted me. The view from the walls of Troy had stunned me.

But the Nile was unlike anything I'd ever experienced.

Setting out from Rhakotis, through the tributaries, so thick, lush, and green. The waters deep and murky, then opening, moving us into the wider waterways; that's what those parts of Lower Egypt are, pathways, roads, of water. And then it does it again, and again. Just when you thought you'd hit the river proper, you would find yourself at another, wider section. Then finally, you end up on the river itself. I still feel dazzled by it. It seems almost like an ocean itself, with its own annual tides.

But the thing that I truly love about the Nile, the thing that caught my eye and that has always drawn me to it, are the monsters.

What monsters am I thinking of? In many ways, they are like the tiny lizards you'd find in the cool parts of a house, or under a shady leaf. Only they are huge, as big as a man, and they look mean, smile cruelly. They have sharp crooked teeth, thick nobbled skin. They swim with ease and even scampering on land are terrifying.

I was, I am, enthralled by them.

They are clearly dangerous, the way they lurk in the river, that grin…

I shiver thinking about it. I know it might sound over-the-top, but they were astonishing to me. The mighty Msh. It might seem strange; that in this new land, in any land, I would be so taken with a single creature.

Something about them captured me on that first journey, and it has never let me go. I have an embalmed one hidden in an alcove, they are very easy to come by where I am, and an effigy of Sobek sits in front of me. Not because I truly believe a god with the head of a crocodile will grant me a good harvest, but because it entrances me.

Why? Why am I drawn to this monster? Why do I still watch them from the safety of distance?

I still do not have an answer for that. Maybe because, to me, this is a legend made flesh; a monster from stories living so close to the realities of life. Its ugliness, its wildness, its danger, and its life in this beautiful river. Perhaps it was what I wanted, what I craved, what I hoped people would see in me. There are other, better, animals to represent freedom, strength, survival – the swan is elegant, the lion a king, the dog loyal, but those are a reminder of home. For me, in Egypt, this one, was love at first sight. It also led me to where I am now, so why I still cling to it is easier to understand.

Leaving Rhakotis was not dramatic, or strained, it didn't happen under cover of darkness, or with bribes. It was straightforward; paying for passage and then being transported like meddlesome cargo. I was not the only one who decided that meeting Odysseus, seeing him leave, was a sign. So, there were a few of us in the low narrow boats the Egyptians favoured.

We didn't have much choice in where we could stop. Our captain had decided the route; we could get off as we wanted, as the boats stopped, but there would be no diversions. Our captain was heading to Naucratis, a city full of Greeks, and that was it. It had been our original destination for that very reason.

That first trip was not technically down the Nile, more across the tributaries of the north. But it was the taste that would come to infect me.

How long did it take? You know by now I cannot count days like that; I've never had cause to. I was also distracted. When not gazing at the river, or searching the banks for those creatures, I was thinking. Trying to think what I needed, wanted, to do next. How I would do it.

I knew I needed to be able to live, comfortably and safely, that I would need to set myself up with a living, a home, food. All the things I'd never been responsible for before; even on that island, others had told me what to do, I'd been part of a community. The idea of having to fend for myself, to live in the world, was one that I now knew I needed to put into practice. I needed to figure out how people did that.

But that wasn't the only thing that occupied my mind as we travelled. As pressing as I knew the practicalities were, I also considered what I wanted, what would make me happy. Freedom, of course, space, to be close to water, away from too many people. And I wanted sky. Does that sound strange? The sky is everywhere, it belongs to everyone. Yet it wasn't until I was on that island, living at Rhakotis, that I realised how confined I'd been. Not to say I'd never been outside, but then I'd been restricted to courtyards, gardens, walls. I was a child of a palace; confined to specific rooms, halls, spaces. Now I'd experienced the vastness that surrounded me.

Perhaps that is the reason I loved the sea, the river, so much; they were so open when my world was so closed.

All this isn't to say that living in the open, under sails and in huts hadn't been hard or that I wanted to repeat the experience. I'm sure sleeping under the stars is wonderful if it's your choice, but a winter with no walls, scavenged firewood, and soup that tastes more like warm water every day was not one I wanted to repeat. That experience had helped me though, had helped forge this new me; this new Lena who knew how to gather firewood and make soup. But the space, with no walls closing in, no whispers behind doors, being able to walk here and there, despite the danger, was a wonder. My desire to not be found drove me away from the sea, but the openness of land, water, sky was everywhere. That's what I wanted.

But how did one achieve those things? That question always crept back into my mind. All I knew was that I couldn't stay in Naucratis. I couldn't stay with my countrymen. I needed to get further away. I also knew I'd need someone to help me.

I had picked up some of the language of Egypt, but not enough to properly navigate my way. And even then, this whole concept of moving on my own was new; exciting but scary. I knew the danger of my naivete, my ignorance; I'd been lucky on the island, we were so shocked and awed, and such a mix of people that no one thought much about me. But now, I would be amongst strangers, in a strange land. Even with my small stash of jewellery, or even because of it, I knew I was at risk. I couldn't do this alone; I'd need to find someone I could trust. Finding someone to help me, finding out how to find someone to help me, was one of my first questions. A daunting task.

Those days of travel came as both a period of relief and of panic. That strange in-between time again, where I was not one thing or another, bound to no place. Even more so than that trip with Paris to Troy; perhaps because then I knew I had very little power over what would happen. Now it was all in my own hands. Or the gods' if you prefer.

Naucratis was bigger than Sparta but not grand like Troy. The temple was the most ornate building, rising above everything else. A common trait in Egypt. I heard snippets of Greek in the crowds around me; but it was odd, old and unknown, understandable but not quite right, and it was surrounded by strange tongues of dialects of so many other places. That was something that I'd come across again and again.

The captain of the boat was kind enough to lead us to a place to stay, for a few coins. Basic, clean, and in the shadows of one of the smaller temples. It seemed to be usual for travellers to stay there. I was relieved when the others who'd travelled with us left to find their own way.

Leaving Rhakotis might not have been strained, but this parting was. I had never grown close to any of them. I'd done my work, learned how to cook and clean and take on the normal chores of a woman. I'd eaten, worked, slept, celebrated, and mourned alongside them. But I'd always kept myself at a distance. I couldn't really trust them. I would only grunt or speak half-truths to their questions. I spent most of my time silent and alone. And they had done the same; the strangeness of tragic companionship – together, but always separate.

Still, they were uncomfortable leaving me, in a strange city, alone. But they did, eventually. I refused to go with them, and they were not going to kidnap me. Besides, they had their own lives to lead, and if they kept me around, someone might have to take responsibility for me.

Then, for the first time in my entire life, I was alone. Truly alone. No one giving me instructions, or shadowing me, or touching me. In that moment, as the other Trojans disappeared from my sight, I felt blind panic. The realisation of how lost I could be, of how terrible a mistake I might be making. It took every fibre of my being, all my strength, not to run after them.

I remember sitting in that room frozen; I could see the dust dancing slowing in the light that slipped through the closed door. Everything seemed to have stopped, except the rush of blood in my head and the pounding of my heart. My body was screaming but the world around me was quiet. I knew I would have to move, to do something, but I didn't know what.

Then the door creaked open. A hinge squeaking, the most normal and every day of sounds, bringing life back to the world and taking me away from myself so I could feel the hard bed beneath me and the currents of air in the room, could smell the dust and heat, could hear the chatter outside.

It was young serving girl. She had brought me water. To drink, to wash, both? I'm not sure. But it brought me back. The girl was jabbering in that strange combination of old Greek, Egyptian, and nonsense words, but she was smiling all the time. When she left, I took a deep breath and stood, feeling my body sway but knowing my feet were firmly on the ground. I drank some water, I washed my face, neck, and wrists. And I went to speak to the owner of the inn, and ask where one could buy some dinner, find cloth, and trade jewellery.

Naucratis

I didn't stay long in Naucratis. I had never intended to; I wanted to get away, because as comforting as it was being surrounded by a familiar patter, recognisable clothes, comforting food, it was also scary. The same fear of discovery haunted me. What if someone here knew me? Unlikely, but not impossible; the world is not that small after all. What if Odysseus had told someone, or one of his shipmates had noticed us talking? What if the new Helen had been uncovered? The closer I was to the Greeks, the closer I was to discovery.

Was I being paranoid? Perhaps. That new fear of being alone morphing into the old one of being discovered. My anxiety at trying to keep myself safe, and survive, leading me to focus on a bigger, less likely danger?

Yet despite this, I stayed in Naucratis longer than I had to. With the help of the Inn owner, her lending me her inquisitive slave boy (for a price of course), I was able to find the places I needed over the next few days, including some fine veils that allowed me to see whilst hiding my scars from others. Once I had that, I found doing any other business to be much easier. The young boy didn't appear to speak a word of Greek, yet he seemed to know exactly what I wanted. The traders were delighted by the fine work of the gold I brought them – I couldn't go to just one, that would raise suspicions - so much so they didn't even melt them down but sold them as they were. I hope the ladies in Naucratis enjoyed them; they'll never know how important their role was in the legend of Troy.

Why did I stay when I wanted to leave, when I knew I needed to leave? When I had everything I needed. I'd even decided where I would go. Memphis was the obvious choice; a city to rival Troy, from what I heard, a place of the living and dead, a point from which to find a new home. Why did I stay when walking the streets would make me sweat or shiver, make my spine crawl, and I'd often rush back to the safety of my lodging, where I could sit in the cool darkness and block out the world.

Perhaps it was allowing myself to adjust, again. Naucratis was another different world to the ones I'd been living in; no huts or makeshift tents here, no grand palaces (though I saw those houses and where the rich lived), but rather a bustling trading town with people from all over. A chance to engage and learn about the world around me, whilst knowing I had a safe, quiet room to run to at dusk.

Just as I'd found more freedom in Troy, I discovered even more freedom in Egypt. Egyptian women had more space to roam, to own, to take control. I do not want to give the impression they the power of men, but they had more freedom that I'd even seen on that island. That was a marvel to me, and I needed to become accustomed to it.

I think both of those were part of it. But I think the bigger part was that I saw myself in the people there. It the comfort of the familiar. People with the same skin, eyes, hair as me. Of course, the Greeks and Egyptians had been living here for years, they had intermarried, made families. But to go from seeing no one similar, except in the curve of a smile in Nest so long ago, to now being in a crowd, was wonderful to me. I do not pretend to know the politics or positions of Naucratis; I didn't want to know. I just enjoyed it. So even while I didn't stay too long, even though I was scared, I was still lulled by that sense of comfort; perhaps it was a bigger threat to my idea of freedom than I realised?

Of course, my enjoyment was limited. I was always behind my veil. My skin might have fit in here, but my scars would never fit in anywhere. That was the price I'd paid. Would I have been thought beautiful in Naucratis? Before the fire melted my skin and hard work changed my body? I don't know. I feel I saw so many beautiful girls and boys there, I even saw someone with skin like mine with beautiful red-brown hair.

Anyway, it doesn't really matter, does it?

I suppose as I walked the streets and surveyed the markets, I was also looking for more than veils and jewellery sellers. For someone who looked like me, more than anyone else. Trade from Naucratis went across the sea, that's how the stories of Troy travelled, and traders went with them, made second homes in faraway lands. I knew it was unlikely, but I suppose I was wondering if a father or family member might be here. One I could join, slip into like a warm bath, and be free and easy and loved and protected.

Again, that lure of comfort. But I knew really that would never happen. We must find that ourselves.

It was a stall in one of the smaller markets that finally spurred me to leave. It sold amulets, small scrappy things mostly, barely discernible for the gods or powers they meant to invoke, made of some metal that would be sure to turn your skin green. As I passed though, something caught my eye. Amongst the scratched and deformed images of Bes and the Eye of Horus, there was a small collection of better ones; finer, more detailed, clearly from a superior craftsman. One of those was of a swan.

My swan brooch, my mother's swan brooch, had travelled with me always. I kept it close, even on the island and at Rhakotis. It was an emblem of so much that had happened to me, perhaps I should have hated it, thrown it away, bestowed it as a charm on the new Helen, but I kept it with me. And here, at this tiny stall in the middle of a market of Naucratis, I had found its twin.

I reached out to touch it without thinking, a mistake at any market I've found, but whilst I know the owner came over to me and started talking, I cannot recall a single thing he said.

I quickly snagged at my veil to get my own, as I used it to keep it in place. Mine was burnished, smoother, duller, but otherwise much the same; graceful neck, strange rendering of the feathers, even small feet tucked away at the bottom.

The only difference was that this seemed almost new, designed more to be worn around the neck or carried, whereas mine had a pin on the back.

The stall holders voice eventually broke through, using that strange version of Greek they spoke here; "Ah music, so lovely. A wonderful way to show your interests. Or just such a pretty thing. And to have a pair, what a treat!"

"What?" I was abrupt, distracted. My mind hadn't yet realised I could ask this man where the amulet came from.

"The swan, a symbol of music, of royalty" the stallholder was small and thin, with a wide smile. His eyes glimmered cheekily, or perhaps just in anticipation of a sale.

"Is it? Is that what it means?" I asked weakly.

"Ah, you are not from Naucratis. I can tell, I can tell. Your voice. You are more Greek. A visitor to our city? Perhaps your husband is a trader, looking for fine things to take home?"

I've often been struck by how easily people can perceive my expression, my reaction to their words, even though my face is covered. The stallholder changed his tack.

"Yes, the swan. They are melodic, they are loved by the pharaoh, they are part of his journey to the afterlife. And they come to Egypt so rarely, only in the winter will you see them. A gift of life when so much of it is hidden."

"And what of this swan?" I asked. "Where did you get it? I'd be interested to meet the craftsman, as you can see, I already have one, and I'd like to see about more."

The stallholders face dropped at this. "I have only a few of these" he admitted, "I purchased them from another. But these are common in Naucratis. This style, this shape. There are many who can fashion more for you, perhaps I could help…"

I shook my head. There was no need.

What was I feeling and thinking then? That this proved my origin? Maybe, though really, it was as mysterious as ever. That I wanted to find out more? Or that it didn't matter, because I never could, that was impossible. I wasn't Helena anymore.

I bought the second swan; for all its finery on that stall, it was still cheap, looped onto a stringy piece of leather. Even then, part of me knew that with a gap of more than 30 years, there was little chance that these two items were from the same hand. Though as I said to Odysseus, and yet.

I still have it, or rather, someone else does.

I left two days after, I wanted to be gone. I knew I had to get away, to find a new home. I needed to go somewhere where I could find a guide, find a home, and be away from the prying eyes of those who knew I must be a lost, wounded woman from Troy.

That swan convinced me that I was finally ready to leave that woman behind.

Memphis & Entef

My first impression of Memphis was that I'd made a terrible mistake.

I do not need to tell you about the grandeur of Egypt. Even now it is a great empire that has risen and fallen half a dozen times. Its history is carved in stone bound to the earth and emblazoned across the sky, dwarfing the great palaces of the Greek and Trojan cities. The great Pharaohs doing battle, wealth flowing in like a second Nile, and all of this on show.

Memphis was huge and busy. It's hard to think of now, I was still adjusting to how my senses worked. It was like nothing I'd ever experienced; I'd never walked the streets of Troy, and Sparta was not a bustling metropolis. I'd spent the last few years in the quiet, living day-to-day, with the sounds of the sea and gentle talk.

Memphis though, made me think of fleeing Troy, the people, the sounds, the smells. I know it was less panicked, that it was the normal ebb and flow of a city, but it made me tremble. It was once I was in the throng of the main city, with its high walls and mud bricks that I really felt it, like the entire place was closing in on me. My veil and headwrap helped protect me from the sun, and the stares of passers-by, and had seemed like nothing in Naucratis, but in Memphis, they suffocated me.

They seemed to catch over my mouth, I found it hard to breath, taking in short gasps which didn't seem to allow air through to my lungs. I could feel my chest hurting, the lack of air invading my body. The fear really came over me then and I had to back away, find some air, some space, away from people.

I managed to find a doorway where I could breathe. I stood facing the corner, hands over my ears, blocking out the noise, the pressure of bodies, the dirt. I focussed on my breathing; I needed to be able to breath, to think, to get away from this place. So, I thought only of that, of breathing in and out. I felt myself calming, my mind clearing.

It was like a bigger version of what I'd felt before; the fear as Troy fell and Menelaus found me, the pressure of Deiphobus' hands on me, freezing and crying as Paris took me from Sparta, the smell of urine in the dark sack from that first terrifying time. It was like it all crashed down on me in one go, like the city somehow drew out every deep and dark moment, brought them all together in my mind, inundating my senses, and I couldn't take it. As much as I was a new person, Lena, the experiences of Helena still sat in my mind.

Even with that knowledge buzzing in my mind, as I calmed down, I started to feel embarrassed. It was just me, in this bright and busy street in Memphis. I should have heeded how I'd felt in Naucratis. A smaller city than Memphis, with familiar voices and people, and yet even there, I'd felt that tingle along my spine, had felt my body react to the world around me. It just had not come through like this.

I felt foolish.

That feeling has never gone away, no matter how often I have one of these moments. In those first few weeks, even years, in Egypt, they were quite common. Being somewhere enclosed or busy would cause them, but they could happen in the quiet too. I told you earlier, a smell, a touch, could spark a memory. Well, they could spark more than that; they could set a fire inside me of desperation and fear.

It has faded as I've gotten older. Perhaps I've forgotten the things that caused it, perhaps I've healed from them. But it still comes. Whenever it happens, has happened, I have followed that path I set in Memphis all those years ago. When I feel overcome, I take myself to a dark, quiet corner, and I focus on my breathing. Sometimes I touch the cool wall, feel the friction beneath my fingers. I most often crawl under my bed; there is something about being surrounded, about being able to dart out of either side, of being far in the back of the house that helps.

But it never really goes away. And I always feel foolish afterwards, no matter what Entef says.

It's probably unsurprising that with this incident, I was drawn back to the docks. They smelt like water and fish and spices, but the water was comforting to me, even with the bustle, it suggested escape. It was busy, but I expected it, and it was a busyness with purpose, easily seen. There was a small temple on the edge of a corner that had caught my eye when I'd arrived; it had a statue of a crocodile-headed man standing outside. I remember I went back and put my hand on the statue, happy that it was there to greet me and ground me. Give me some feeling of permanence. The crocodile would never be afraid of something as silly as a crowded street, they'd never been afraid of anything.

I knew I had to find the boarding rooms I'd been told about before dark. I already knew I couldn't stay here. Memphis would hide me, but it was too much. I'd wanted to be away from the sea, from the Greeks, from the past, but I wanted sky and space.

I've been to Memphis many times since then, and I've enjoyed it. I have a better sense of the streets and the places to go, and I've had a strong and comfortable arm to help guide me. I always make sure to pass by that temple though. To nod thanks and to place my hand on that statue, a benediction, to ground myself; as though each time I do it, my sense of self reasserts.

It was there, next to that statue, as my heart slowed and my mind calmed, that I met Entef.

Ahhh, we come to it. I mentioned him long ago; it was his idea to write this all down. He's seen all of this and yet he's still here. You already know where this is going, but I should tell you how we got here.

Entef's skin is dark, a lot darker than mine, and his head is completely bald, except for when he wears a wig. He was a scribe, and he speaks many languages fluently, including Greek, or at least, that strange, old-fashioned Greek everyone here seemed to speak. Otherwise, we would never have met, would never have made a life together. When we first met, I saw a tall man with a pot belly. He was handsome I suppose, with his dark skin and rich brown eyes, lined with kohl, but that is something I only noticed later. He dressed as a scribe, though one travelling so also had a cloak and a large bag with him. At the time I was searching his eyes, trying to decide if I should trust him. I've often found people with kind eyes when you meet them are actually hard as stone, but those with hard eyes are the ones with heart underneath. His eyes gave nothing away.

I'm not sure what Entef saw when he first laid eyes on me. I want to ask him, but he's dozing, and I don't want to disturb him, even though he would say he doesn't mind. Factually, he would have seen a veiled, travel-worn foreigner with a dirty dress and clearly lost, in so many ways. So why did he come over? Why did he see me, looking up at that statue, and decide he should talk to me?

He once told me it was because of the way I held myself, another time he said it was because I was at his favourite place in Memphis, and once again, that a fortune teller had told him to look out for a veiled woman. He does like stories, and playing with words, though never to be cruel. I think the reason is easier than that. It was because he thought I might need his help, because he knew I was an easy mark for the dangerous men in Memphis, he thought I was lost.

In short, I think the real reason he came over to me is simply because he is a kind man.

He has had his own hardships; a drunken father, a brother who took his share of the family land. And he was, is, cut. Entef is a eunuch; not by his own choice, but because it was decided. He lives with the impact of that; his limbs do not grow the same, his voice is boyish, he cannot father children. Entef's story is his own, and I do not wish to tell it here. But I think you need to know this, it's part of who he is, why he is who he is, and why I love him.

When he first spoke to me, I admit I nearly ran. I was taken by surprise, I didn't understand what he said, and I was still recovering from my panic. But I managed to still myself, and responded without thinking, probably saying I didn't understand. Then I found that he spoke Greek, which made everything much easier. For me at least.

I'm not sure I trusted him then, even as he showed me a place to stay, and listened as I explained what I wanted, what I needed, whilst trying to reveal as little as possible – about my position, my new found wealth (strategically hidden in my clothes, bags, veils, and anywhere else so should the worst happen, I would at least be able to survive). I didn't trust him when he said he would return the next day and help me. For a fee, of course; kindness only goes so far.

But Entef was as good as his word, as he always is, I've found. He returned, he tried to explain to me the laws in Egypt, the rules that needed to be followed, how purchasing and owning worked, what would be needed and so on. As a scribe, he had become familiar with these things. But I didn't understand him. I had little concept of what he spoke about; I'd never truly owned anything or needed to think about these things before. Add to that the strangeness of the rules in Egypt, and I realised in talking to him, I was truly lost. I just knew that I wanted a place to live and that it must be away from this city.

So, we started looking. Looking for a small property. Somewhere safe, but spacious, a place I could own but could also live off.

Oh, but the luck of meeting Entef; perhaps the gods were watching after all. When I think back on that time I shiver at my good fortune, at how it could have gone so wrong. A wrong step, a turn down a different street, and I'd probably have been found floating face down in the Nile, instead of being able to lounge beside it 30 years later. I touch my little Sobek statue, I bring my hand up to my swan brooch, grounding myself, thanking the world for allowing me this.

I later learned Entef had just lost out on a position, one that would have secured his future. This after travelling himself to Memphis, from far in the south, and giving up a position there. One he would not be welcome back to. So, we were both in the same situation, though to me he had seemed so confident and in charge. Entef was also looking for something, was alone and needed to find a new way, and when he found me, it seemed at first like a way to help himself. Entef is kind, but he is also practical.

It took weeks, and much travelling, which ate into my fund. Nowhere was quite right. And it was hard to decide how it was wrong. I shan't bore you with the details of that search, mostly because I can no longer remember them. Even that important time with Entef fades slightly, overtaken by the years of familiarity that have come since.

It was over that time of travelling, that I spoke with Entef, got to know him. I didn't tell him much about me; he guessed I was a survivor of Troy, that I was a noble woman. But he didn't know the city, only knew the stories. The questions he asked were easy to lie about.

I think he knew I lied about some of it. He never pushed or pressed, he accepted what I told him, and once I knew more about him, that made sense.

When he first saw my face unveiled, he was taken aback; people often are, so it's not the first moments they see me that tell me about them, it's the moments after that. Entef quickly recovered, he returned to normal immediately, and looked at me as he looked at everyone. The same as he had looked at me when veiled. That felt so wonderful, to be looked at in that way; I've already told you of the power and pressure of being looked at whilst beautiful, and the loneliness and strangeness of being ignored when ugly. To be looked at just as everyone else is, that was special; Entef probably had no idea how much that meant to me, and how much it played into my feelings for him. He only ever mentioned my face to check that I was well as we travelled, to offer ointment from an apothecary he knew, which did help as I learned the Egyptians are very skilled in medicine.

At the end of our meeting, when I had showed him my face, I asked him if he could stand it, if he really wanted to be seen with me.

"I see no reason not to see or be seen with you," had been his response.

Maybe it was just a clever thing to say. Maybe it was the abused feeling pity for the abused. Or maybe it was just his kindness. Looking back, I think it was the first thing about him to pierce my heart.

I try not to think of what would have happened if we had not met that day. But it's a question that niggles, as so many do. Would we have met the next day? I was looking for someone to help and he was looking for something to do, after all. We would have ever met in such a city as Memphis? Would I have found this life? Probably not. He would have found another position, not one he wanted, but one he hoped would give him the opportunity for more in the future. I would have found someone else, maybe been swindled, or killed. I don't know if it was fate, luck, or the crocodile god, but if one thing had to go right in my life, I'm glad it was finding Entef.

Sedet

Of course, I wanted somewhere near water. Easily done, since almost anywhere in Egypt worth living would be on the Nile. But I was reluctant to return north, or to cling too closely to the river. I thought of the lush, wide tributaries of Lower Egypt, and I knew I wanted something like that. But I couldn't go back.

I think Entef gleaned some of the reasons why; my face, being away from Greece and the ramifications of the war made a lot of sense. Some want to stay close, wallow in tragedy, but that would never have been me. So, he suggested we cross the border into the south, Upper Egypt, the Land of Reeds. He thought we might find what I was looking for in Sedet.

He was right, but don't tell him I said that. His head is big enough as it is.

Sedet seemed even more lush than what I'd already seen of Egypt, it was like the Nile valley writ small and concentrated. There were farms and grains. It was rich and modern, with new buildings and a heathy population. It had the towns and culture, but it also had space. As soon as I started walking around it, I knew this is where I would live the rest of my days. It didn't matter what it involved; I would do it.

There was more of course, I felt like I could fit in here. Not my scars of course, they would always stand out, single me from the crowd, divert eyes and leave a trail of whispers. But in other ways, I fit in. Much like Naucratis, there was nothing about me to comment on. I will never know if my father was from Naucratis or Kush, was a god or a sailor, but it felt like he could be from this place. So, this was where I could be, and not be alone.

It was Entef who found the house; small, roomy, with its own plot; space to grow, brew beer, keep some animals. Close enough to the water to be able to keep a boat, with a view. On the edge of a village with no name.

By that point, I'd seen a dozen such properties. But this felt right. Not only because of Sedet. The village was small, but it did have a temple, a small one, inconsequential, and rudimentary. It was to the crocodile god Sobek, to encourage a good harvest, to protect the people from the monsters in the Nile. A sign? Fate at work again? Or just

Entef, being exceptionally good? It doesn't matter, the place sang to me.

And I should say that Entef was exceptionally good. I'd seen that throughout our journey; he seemed to know the ins-and-outs of everything, everything that would make purchasing and selling easier. I had been feeling sorry that he was working so hard, doing so much, whilst I simply looked and thought and then said no. He would tell me over dinner that was fine, then he'd make some joke and we'd laugh and talk, and dream about what life would be like on this fantasy land.

As good as he was, when it came to this property, my only question was the price.

It was high.

But if it had been lower, would Entef and I have talked so openly that evening, as we ate bread and meat together on the shore? Another niggling question, another twist of life.

I had never loved my husbands, but I had affection for them, I had consented, even wanted, to marry them. They were the fathers of my children; the men I thought I would spend my life with. You cannot live like that and not have some feeling. But I'd never had love, never been in love; I had never really wanted it. I had Nest, even when she was gone, I still had her. And then I had my children. The idea of loving a man, being in love with him, seemed…beyond me. Especially when I thought about my reaction to the mere idea of those intimacies, the touching, caressing, thrusting, I could feel the distaste bubbling inside me. That feeling has increased with age. What once I could at least withstand for the sake of men, for the sake of the world I lived in, had turned completely to revulsion.

As I sat with Entef, and considered how close we were to the end of our journey together, I felt sad. I felt a crack in my heart like I hadn't felt before. My heart had been broken by Nest, by my boy's deaths, by the devastation of Troy, but those were the raw grief of things that had happened, that could not be undone. This was different; more like heartbreak I suppose, like the sadness of something passing, opportunities missed. I had never really thought of myself as having many opportunities before, so this was something new. I supposed in that moment that I had gotten used to him. We would talk as we travelled, tell each other stories; he would explain the world around me, and I would marvel and ask more. He even started to show me how to write. I felt comfortable with him, the only person who came close was Nest, but certainly no man.

It was him who suggested a new plan though.

"We should buy this place" it was simple, straightforward. He made it sound like a purely business proposal, but my heart stilled jumped.

"Together?"

He wouldn't meet my eyes as he spoke, that was unusual. "As partners. I have some of my own money; it was supposed to help me get situated. It's not a lot, but it would make up the difference, and allow for the purchase of seed and animals."

I didn't respond. He said partners, that could mean so many things – business, friendship, something more. In all our time talking, neither of us had revealed our relationships; he had asked me once if I was a widow, and I said yes. That was the truth, or at least, partly the truth. It all felt so confusing and weighted.

I was thinking of what to say, but he took my silence another way.

“Never mind. It is a foolish idea. We will find another place for you.” He was turning, turning away from the fire, away from me, readying to stand and walk away. I had to do something.

“No” I almost shouted the word. “No, please. I like the…idea. But maybe too much” I looked away as I said it. I hoped he would understand the words. I didn’t want to make a scene, and I didn’t want to say it out loud. My courage failed me in this moment, I didn’t know how to parse these feelings into words. I hoped he would understand this code, and either accept or reject in kind.

Also, as much as I enjoyed his company, as much as I liked the idea of staying with him, I was only blind in one eye. I knew how I looked. Being gelded did not stop a man from appreciating beauty or being repulsed by ugliness. He had been kind, normal, around me and my scars, but how much could that really mean? Kindness is not the same as love.

I also knew how I felt about physical intimacy. Yes, I knew he was cut, but I also know this means different things. I hadn’t exactly enquired about what remained. Men have varying tastes, and who knew what his might be. And yet, the idea of a partner, of someone to hold, someone to be with as a companion, made my heart leap. Even the idea of partnership just in ownership and business, in friendship, made me feel pleased and safe. Especially if that partner was Entef.

I waited for his response.

He stayed quiet, and then gently took my hand. I turned to face him as he did so. He was smiling. Entef has several different smiles, I've learned. He has a wide one, all teeth showing, for when he is amused and laughing; a thin contemplative one for a job well done; he has an open one which lights up his whole face when he is truly happy; and he has one just for me, this one is small, quiet, almost secret. But I see it. That evening, I saw it for the first time.

We know what would usually happen at this moment in the story, declarations of love, a kiss, more. But that wasn't what this was. This wasn't passion, it never has been, this was companionship, liking each other, being partners. We didn't say we loved each other, not for a long time to come, but even that love, it was solid and comfortable.

Yet, both of us, still needed to explain so much to the other. We had discussed a lot of things, but the ability and desire for intimacy is not something that had come up between us.

It was Entef who went first; he tried to explain his member was still there, but no more, that he could not, did not want to use it. I remember smiling at him then; not a big grin, but what I hoped was a smile of reassurance. I tried to honour his honesty and faith in me by telling him that I was not interested in physical sex, but I'm not sure he fully understood. I had no cuts or anything else physical to stop me. He had to take it on faith that I was being honest.

Trust is a hard thing in this life. But it's something Entef and I had from the beginning. I think that more than anything is why we loved each other.

I did feel one pang though. I didn't want sex, but I realised this meant I would never have another child. My children were gone. Even to the ones still living, I knew I would never be their mother again. I suppose I hadn't really considered that. That this meant I would never be pregnant or give birth to a child. I admit, it was something that gave me a moment of pain, a twist in my heart, but it was not strong enough to stop me. After all, I'd lost all my children, I didn't want to go through that again. Besides, there are other ways to have a child.

Truth was something that came out over time. The one thing I wasn't honest with him about on the banks of the Nile that night was who I was. He knew me as Lena, lady of Troy. Though even that was difficult as the Egyptians do not understand the letter 'L', whereas Greek is full of them. Instead, he called me what was easiest for him to say, Ena. Similar, but not the same. So that's who I became, and it's funny to think that as my name diminished, I grew.

I didn't tell him who I was until sometime after we were married. Why when we had such trust? Because I'd been running away. I wasn't ready to bring Helena with me just yet. It was about me, not Entef.

He found me one day, in our little home, holding my swan brooch.

It was the day after a party of traders had come through our small village. They were telling tales, including tales of me. But then they told another. About the mad wife Clytemnestra, who had murdered her husband in revenge for his sacrifice of their daughter, and who had herself been murdered in turn by her son. A Greek tragedy, as the new saying goes.

It had happened years earlier, but it was the first I had heard of it. I knew enough of songs and tales to know that it wouldn't all be true, but the talk of her actions, her death…It hit me. Because I knew that sounded just like what my sister would do.

I had thought of seeking her out, getting a message to her. There was a distant dream of her joining us in Egypt, us living together again, as sisters. But something always held me back. There was the fear of ruining that dream; the thing that holds so many of us back from doing what we want. But there was something more. Fear for myself? Fear for the life I was building? Fear that there was no longer a Nest to reunite with? You probably think it silly, that I could know, in my soul, that a sister I'd not seen for more than 20 years was dead. But when I heard those stories, my heart was not surprised, even as I grieved. And then there was that scream I'd heard so long ago in Troy, that still sounded in my head from time to time. I knew Nest was gone.

After hearing those stories, I had gone straight home and pulled out the brooch. I wept as I stroked it and thought of those two little girls in Sparta; of the laughter and promise they had, all that had happened to them, and how their stories had ended.

Entef found me weeping, and I knew I had to tell him everything.

Did he believe me? Maybe not at first. It's a great and terrible story. Do you even believe me? And this ending makes it more unbelievable, doesn't it? How can it end like this? But he understood I was telling some type of truth, that I was that person. That great and terrible woman.

I remember how he held me. We were always affectionate with each other, we both craved touch. But this felt different. He was holding me to protect me, to support me. He'd never had to do that before, I'm not sure anyone really had.

"You are my Ena" was all he'd said.

"And what about this?" I'd asked, showing him the brooch.

He'd smiled, and took it from me, fastening it to my dress; "Ena can wear a brooch to honour the past, and still be Ena in the present."

As I gazed at him in that moment, I knew what I wanted to do. I went quickly to a small bag and pulled out the swan amulet I'd found in Naucratis. I put it into Entef's hand.

"For you" I said, softly, "see how it matches, newer but a match. You have one, and I have one."

"The past, the present, and the future" he smiled, that smile just for me.

He was right.

Life for 30 years

This has been my life for the past three decades.

Entef and Ena; a strange couple on the edge of a village, nice enough but quiet.

Our marriage ceremony was small, foreign to me, and more for legal reasons than anything. We knew we would not have children, but women in Egypt can hold property, so it was important to do. He oversees the business, the farm work, manages accounts and trade. I look after our garden, I sit at the loom, I brew the beer, and oversee the staff. There are no slaves in this house, I've learned that much at least.

He has taught me to speak Egyptian, to write out the scribbles that mirror the words we say. I have taught him about the customs of Sparta and Troy. He finds them as strange and exotic as I find him and the ways of Egypt.

Little has happened to us; we live, we work, we love. We sleep and eat and go to the same markets and talk to the same people, and in the evenings, we often walk by the river, or sit in our garden, holding hands, and enjoy the quiet.

We have needed help in our business, especially as we got older. Entef was already a decade older than me, and his eyesight started to fade quite soon. We found a young farmhand, a lost little slave-boy. Mesu; clever, eager, cheeky, and alone in the world. Sometimes I look at him, and for a moment I see my sons. For a while when he first came, I couldn't look at him at all, that flash in my mind made it too painful. But in time that has faded. He's grown tall and lean; I sometimes think there is something of Paris in his face. But he is as dark as me, with high cheekbones, full lips, and eyes like the Nile. We had not planned it, but soon enough, Entef was teaching him as one would a scribe, and I was cooking for him as one would a close friend. We were both treating him as our son. That is what he became.

He is our son, for all intents; we have taught him and raised him. I'm not stupid, I know he must have been born around the same time as my youngest son, that I see Paris in him, and my heart grows and hurts around him. He was not a replacement, but I have always enjoyed my children, and Entef has his kind disposition. Perhaps we were easily placed to fall into adoption, but why should we not, when there is a child who needs love and people to give it? So, we did it anyway, and have been happy. Entef saw to it that Mesu became ours legally, not as a slave but as family. When we are gone, he will take on the farm. Right now, he lives in the extension we added on to our house during the good years. He's just been married, and soon there will be a baby. I am excited. I haven't held a baby in so long.

I don't want to write too much of Mesu. As with Entef, his story is not mine to tell, and he still has a long life ahead of him. He will most likely be the one to find this and read it after I am gone. I hope he knows how much I love him, and that I hope he has a good life.

It does make me wonder about my own children though, my grandchildren. I hear some stories of them, though they are not as well-known as their parents and grandparents. I can tell, the stories, they mix people up; some of the stories must be about the new Helena of Troy's children with Menelaus, some are about those he had with another woman. For my own children, I hear stories of Hermione's marriages; that she is strong and has managed to secure a husband she wanted. I hope she is happy. Aethiolus I do not hear much about; he should have been king of Sparta. I fear he has gone. I include him in my prayers with Nest, just in case.

That might sound callous, dismissing my children so easily. But it has been a long time, and they were never considered mine to begin with. When I was married to Paris, I thought I would never see them again. I mourned them then. It's all I could do, and it's all I can do now.

Perhaps the biggest sign of the changes in my life has been my jewellery; I wear my swan brooch still, even at night, but little else. I admit, I still have a few pieces hidden here or there, safely packed away for a rainy day, but my wardrobe is no longer a treasury. If I stood before Priam now, I'd have very little to barter with. Not that anyone would want to barter for an old, scarred, Egyptian countrywoman.

So, my life in Sedet has continued, it's been, still is, happy. Though, I am still weighed down by those thoughts of the past. They never entirely left me. It's why I'm recording it all here.

Do you want to hear about these years spent between finding this home and writing this down? About the years when the flood did not come, or when we had abundance? The years of planting, caring, growing, and reaping? When Entef's eyes were so bad we knew he wouldn't be able to see for much longer? How the hearing in my nubbin ear disappeared completely? When Mesu drank too much beer with his friends and vomited over my lettuce patch? About how Entef and I would just sit quietly together in the evenings just holding hands, and sharing the stories of our worlds? How we would joke and smile?

There are no more stories of heroes or wars in this tale. Just life being lived. We have grown old here, we are simple, and except for my scars, no one thinks I am anything but a moderately wealthy old woman with my old, blind husband, and my charming, handsome adopted son. Some of them may not even remember Mesu is adopted anymore; he is simply our son.

Yet still, sometimes at night, I dream I am on the walls of Troy, or I'm back in that room, Menelaus' sword to my throat, or I'm in that sack headed to Athens. And I wake up drenched in sweat, a scream in my chest. But Entef is there, and he brings me back to the present.

Does it seem strange to you, that I won't go into details? I've spent rolls of parchment telling you about my life, describing intimate moments of things half-remembered, berating people whose deeds have gone down in history, and yet I won't tell you about the life I have lived here.

I just don't feel I can. It's not nearly as interesting as the rest, and it has been much the same. It has been the sway of life. I haven't much spoken of the sway of life here, or how the seasons affected what I wore or the festivals. Because you already know the sway of life, everyone does.

I have my sky and my river, my garden and my loom, my partner, and my family. Maybe this doesn't seem like a lot. Or perhaps you read this and think that this is exactly what I had before; that when I was living in palaces all I had was my own interests and my own place, and it's my own fault for not revelling in it. For not enjoying the power and prestige and wealth that I had.

You might be right.

But in this small farm in Sedet, I found happiness.

Everyone around here is even accustomed to my face now, so I generally pass by unnoticed when I leave home. There are sometimes some jeers, if the beer has been flowing, or children are feeling especially mean-spirited. The maids who help me certainly whisper, though I think they are intrigued as to how it happened, and are kind, attentive otherwise. And now I am a very old lady, you can barely tell the scars from the weather-beaten wrinkles.

I do think of the people I left behind. Nest and my children come to my mind every day; how can they not? And Menelaus. Entef can always tell when they are on my mind; he used to say my eyes change, they become sad in a deep way, though now he says it's in my voice, and he will wrap his arms around me and just stands with me until I let go.

It is hard for him to do that now. He mostly sits in the shade outside. His legs are not what they used to be and with his sight gone, there's not much he can do. He often jokes that we only have one good eye among us! And when he does, I laugh and hold his hand and we sit together as I use our one good eye to tell him what's happening. Our favourite time to do this is just before dawn, when it is quiet and fresh, where we sit overlooking our little farm, and watch the world be born anew, praising Amun.

VI. The Ending

I am putting off finishing. I don't know how to finish. Yes, I'm old and happy. I still have a little life left in me, so I know the story isn't completely over. But the writing of it must be. I wish I had something more dramatic to end it on; but I'm not dying, no more than anyone else, no one has jumped out of a doorway declaring they know who I am, and neither Entef nor I have broken our vows.

As I sit here, thinking about this ending, I can't help but look at the beginning. I look back over the reams of scroll, so long and yet so short for my life, for any life. Or at least part of it. The parts I can remember, or care to remember.

I think of the way my life, all lives, are formed. They say the three sisters weave out lives together, and if so, then for mine they used a lot of thread. There are so many chances missed, others taken, coincidences, and careful plans. So many moments in my life that could have taken me down a different path, far away from where I am now. I suppose that is true of every life, blessed or cursed, and we don't see it until we near the end.

I wonder what I've left out. What questions you still have unanswered. Do you think me shallow and cruel; do you dislike that I don't spend so much time speaking of my children, or that I barely mention Nest once she left? Are you annoyed that I didn't look further for my father, examine myself and my looks more? Or do you feel short-changed by my descriptions of life after Troy; would you like a breakdown of every step I've taken?

Does it matter to me if you have these feelings? Does it really matter to you?

As I look back, I find myself lingering on that first question, the one that started this rambling. The first piece of chance that directed my life.

How does a woman give birth to an egg?

She doesn't. The physicality of it alone shows that. But people believed it, or said they did, and now I'm here.

Perhaps that is the last question you have for me: how am I now? How do I feel about the life I've lived?

When I look back, I am neither pleased nor angry at what happened to me. I had moments of great joy and great sorrow, of fear and love, I learned so much, and lost the same. This is how it is; I do not thank the bad moments for making me who I am, I wish they had not happened, but that's not how life works. Life happens and we are all forged in its flames. It's only that these things are what happened to me. Throughout my life, I have been so many different things, I've been different women.

Helena. Lena. Ena.

But now, at the end, I am me.

Printed in Great Britain
by Amazon

60384522R00129